The King's Treasure

One Task, Book Three

Geneva Gordon

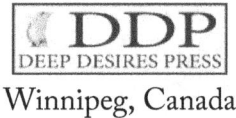
DDP
DEEP DESIRES PRESS
Winnipeg, Canada

Developmental editor: Craig Gibb
Proofreader: Francisco Feliciano

Published March 2024 by Deep Desires Press, an imprint of Story Perfect Inc.

Deep Desires Press
PO Box 51053 Tyndall Park
Winnipeg, Manitoba R2X 3B0
Canada

Visit http://www.deepdesirespress.com for more scorching hot erotica and erotic romance.

The King's Treasure

PROLOGUE

The two armies faced each other, separated by the battlefield. King Simon Lassiter of Moregane, accompanied by Tig, his Aide de Camp, rode to the center of the field to meet with the King of Gretna and his general.

Tig lifted her leg over Juno's back and vaulted to the ground. She was dressed in a black lacquered breast plate, which had the figure of a demon with red eyes hammered into it, and black leather pants that tightly hugged her figure. Her blonde hair was pulled into a ponytail at the top of her head. A black cloak hung from her shoulders. Griffin, a huge gray dog, stood beside her.

Jossie, the Gretnan advisor, watched her approach with admiration in his eyes. She knew she was a sight to behold. She strode up to him, entering his space, staring into his eyes. The dog followed her, approaching him. Griffin suddenly slowed, dropped into a hunting crouch, and approached him, teeth bared, snarling. He thought he had more to fear from the dog than he did from this beautiful woman dressed for war.

"What are you looking at, ass-wipe?" Tig challenged Jossie. Griffin growled.

Jossie cleared his throat. "Madam, on behalf of the King of Gretna, I offer you and your men immunity if you will walk away and concede victory to us." He spoke politely, reasonably.

"That's very considerate but it's not going to happen." Tig took a moment to look at Simon. He nodded his head at her. Tig tsked and turned back to Jossie. "I am being forced to offer you your lives if you turn the fuck around and just leave."

"Our goal is to take Moregane and incorporate it into the kingdom of Gretna. We hope that we can accomplish that peacefully, but we are certainly willing to do it by force." Again, with the reasonable tone, this time with a smirk, implying perhaps she was unreasonable if she refused. She was infuriated by his attitude.

"My goal is to wipe your sorry ass off the face of the earth," she spat at him, "and, by the way, it's going to hurt."

Tig had him at a loss. By this time in the conversation, he was certainly expecting concessions offered, negotiations started. She offered nothing. He turned to his King. His King looked at Simon.

"My military advisor suggests that you and your army should leave Moregane. We will, of course, escort you to the border, but you will be allowed to leave unharmed," Simon said.

Jossie addressed Tig again, "We have fought our way here and arrived victorious. We intend to continue through Moregane to Sandria and take Sandria before continuing south."

"Just fucking try it, asshole." Her eyes burned with rage, Tig stepped closer, forcing Jossie to take a step back.

Again, Jossie looked to his King.

"My military advisor says we are ready to defend Moregane," Simon advised the invader.

The King looked to Jossie. He looked annoyed.

"We outnumber you," Jossie stated. "Our men are seasoned warriors, we—"

"That's what the last group of rebels said. Our crows are still feasting on their bodies. You want to do this, then do it, and stop posturing. I want you to know one thing though. I will be coming for you, you cocksucker. You and your men will be sorry you ever entered Moregane…but you won't live long enough to regret it."

Simon looked at the invading king and shrugged his shoulders. "We will not negotiate." He stood and mounted his horse, waiting for Tig.

Tig took a step closer to Jossie, their noses almost touching. "I'll be seeing you real soon," she said before turning on her heel. Griffin snapped at Jossie, then turned to follow Tig. She mounted Juno and turned Juno to ride beside Simon, Griffin trotting at Juno's heels.

From her peripheral vision, Tig saw Jossie release a tense breath. That had been intense for him she thought, but she knew he believed every word that had come from her mouth. But she also knew he would watch for her. There was a hardness in his eyes that told her he would teach her a thing or two before he killed her. Or tried to, anyway.

Tig looked over at Simon as they rode back to their army. "When this is done, I am going to fuck you for days."

He laughed. "Let's get this done then, Tig. You can count on having my full attention for as long as it takes."

She spurred Juno forward. Time to get serious.

Tig and Simon were leading an army of strong, well-trained warriors. Tig had assumed control of training the men after Clarence's execution for treason, for partaking in the plot to make her disappear. She had taught them everything she knew: fitness, nutrition, sword play, throwing stars, and martial arts. She had instilled in them honor and loyalty to themselves, their country, their King, and her. They were proud to be the Moregane army. They were considered elite fighters, and dangerous. Mercenaries, soldiers from other armies, and sons of nobles all came to be trained by Tig. They gladly swore their fealty to Simon for the opportunity to fight with her. They may be outnumbered by the Gretnans but each one of her warriors were worth two, or more, of theirs.

Their men had been informed of the game plan before they arrived on the field. They were prepared for what was coming and were anxious to fight. Tig and Simon rode to them and turned their horses to face the invaders. Tig pulled her sword, raised it above her head, then brought it down, pointing at the enemy. She signaled Juno who jumped forward. Tig screamed her war cry and charged toward the other army, her men behind her.

Jossie and the King of Gretna had no sooner returned to their front line when Tig's war cry sounded. The King bolted for the rear of his army; Jossie spun his mount around and began his charge.

The two forces clashed in the middle of the field. Steel

met steel. Men fell. Screams cut the air. Blood flowed and spurted. Lives were lost. The King of Gretna retreated, taking what was left of his army with him. Jossie lay at Tig's feet, his eyes staring blankly at the sky, Griffin stood at her side, his muzzle stained with blood.

There was nothing romantic about standing amid the aftermath of a battle. The stink of death consisted of blood, sweat, and human waste. The air was filled with the sound of men dying, moaning and crying out in pain, or calling for their mothers, their loved ones or their gods. And yet the victors were filled with the exhilaration of a fight well fought and the elation of having survived.

Tig surveyed the carnage. She had lost warriors and she felt that loss, but she was alive and so were a great number of her men. She scanned those still standing, looking for Simon. She didn't see him. She started back toward their staging area, stopping along the way to slay those too close to death to survive, or to assist those she could.

Hours later, she entered camp, still looking for Simon. He was not there. She called her officers. They regrouped and returned to the battlefield, searching for him.

Tig found him. He was in the middle of the field, half hidden by the dead surrounding him. She pulled the bodies off of him. He lay still. She dropped to her knees, calling for help. She pulled his armor off, looking for wounds, but found none. She checked his pulse, pulled his eyelid up. He was alive but unresponsive. Men gathered around her. Together they gently lifted him and that's when the source of his injury was revealed. He had fallen and struck his head on a rock. Tig knew the seriousness of such a seemingly-innocuous injury. She knew that death had been a possibility and she was thankful that Simon had survived. She also knew that brain damage was a possibility and that would not be known until he regained consciousness.

Five days later Simon had still not woken. They were back in Vestary. Simon was in his chamber, attended to by the doctor around the clock.

Tig carried on as she always did. Training her men and herself. Visiting with the injured. Assisting the families of the fallen. Her mind, though, was with Simon. She was worried. She spent every spare moment with him, sitting by his bedside, assisting in his care, talking to him and finally demanding, then begging, him to wake up.

CHAPTER 1

On the seventh day, Tig had just finished morning exercises. She stood by the pail and lifted a ladle of water, pouring it over her head. It ran down her face, darkening her tunic, running between her breasts and pooling at the waistband of her shorts. She lifted another ladle of water and drank deeply.

"Lady Tig." A page appeared in front of her.

She put down the ladle and wiped the back of her hand across her mouth. "Yes."

"The King is awake."

Her heart leapt. "When did he wake up?"

"This morning. The doctor has sent me to get you."

"Thank you," she said.

She entered the castle and strode down the hall toward Simon's chamber. She pushed open the doors and saw him sitting on the chest at the foot of his bed. She smiled.

"Simon, at last. You owe me a fu—"

He looked at her. He scanned her from head to toe and back again. A look of utter disgust entered his eyes.

Tig stopped in her tracks.

"You're wet," he said, annoyance tingeing his words.

"Yes."

"Yes?" Now he looked insulted.

"Yes."

"Is there anything you want to add to that?" Is he speaking to her as if she were a child?

"Yes, I'm wet?"

"That's all?" Yes, that is the tone he would use with an idiot.

"Let's just stop this now." Tig had had enough of this guessing game. "What is it you're expecting me to say? Tell me and I'll say it."

"You will address me as Your Highness, or Sire, if you wish."

She rolled her eyes at him, which only made him more annoyed. "Okay."

"Okay?"

"Okay, Your Highness."

"Who are you?"

"Who do you think I am Simo…Sire?"

He studied her again, his gaze going to the knife at her waist. He forced himself to stand. "I have no idea who you are, Madam. I can only assume by your lack of clothing that you are a whore. Perhaps the castle idiot, as you do not seem to be aware of court etiquette." He paused in his assessment of her. "Why are you wandering the castle dressed as you are? Why you felt free to barge into my chamber and call me by my name is beyond me."

"You think I'm a whore?" Her hand rested on her blade and her eyes flashed with annoyance. "Who are you?"

She was quite beautiful. Even more so in anger. "I am Simon Lassiter, recently prince of Moregane. I have just been informed of the death of my brother Cameron. Now I am King of Moregane. But you know that."

"I do know that," she confirmed. Wariness came into her eyes.

"You said I owe you something. What do I owe you?"

The question caught her off guard and she clearly struggled to come up with an answer.

"You owe me a fiver," she blurted out.

"And what would I owe you money for," he demanded.

"We had a bet, Sire. I won."

"And what bet was that?"

"Our bet was who would end up in a coma for seven days. You lost. I won. You owe me five."

"You joke?"

"I wish it were a joke, but, no. There is nothing funny here."

"Very well. See my secretary tomorrow. He will pay you. My debt will be settled."

"Fine." The woman turned to leave.

"Madam," he called her back.

She turned. "Yes."

"Your name," he demanded.

"Tig. My name is Tig, Sire."

"Tig." He lingered over her name, so strange and unique. "Next time I see you, I expect you will be properly clothed."

She looked at him as if he were an idiot. That irked him. He stared at her. "You may leave now."

She turned and stormed out of his room. Simon felt relieved and disappointed at the same time.

He had awakened mere hours ago after apparently having been in a coma for seven days. He knew who he was and he knew where he was. He recognized the doctor but was surprised to learn that he seemed to have lost years of his life.

He had been distraught to learn that his father and his brother, Cameron, were dead. He realized at that moment as well that he was now King. The doctor told him that that was all he needed to know for now, that particulars would be provided over time if his memory did not return.

He was dealing with those facts, trying to reconcile himself to his loss and his new position when that woman had stormed into his room. Her easy familiarity with him struck him as odd. He would have to learn more about her.

CHAPTER 2

After leaving Simon's chamber, Tig went straight to the surgery.

"I was expecting you, Lady Tig," the doctor said when he saw her. "You have questions, I'm sure."

"Yes, I have questions. What's wrong with Simon?"

"The head injury he suffered seems to have erased his memory of the past five or six years. He knows who he is and he knows where he is. He recognized me. But key events have been erased; his father's death, his brother's death, to name a few."

"When will his memory return?"

"There is no way to know when or even if his memory will return. I'm sorry, Madam."

Tig left the surgery in turmoil. Simon did not remember her. He did not remember *them*. The look he had given her had been one of utter disgust. He thought she was a whore. She was certainly not about to tell him that he loved her when it seemed he could not even stand the sight of her.

She would wait and hope that his memory returned. She would not give up on him. He had not given up on her when she had been suffering and in turmoil. The thought that perhaps his memory would not return popped into her mind but she quickly pushed it away. He had to remember them. How could he not?

She went to the stables to saddle Juno and continue training with the men in the afternoon.

There was a knock at Simon's chamber door.

"Enter," he commanded.

Mrs. Abbot came in carrying a tray with a bowl of stew and some bread. "So good to see you awake, Sire," she gushed. "We were all worried about you."

"Thank you, Mrs. Abbot," he responded. "I am glad to see you too. Is that your famous mutton stew?"

"It is, indeed, Sire, your favorite."

"You spoil me, but I'm glad for it. I'm starving." Simon sat at a table in the corner of his chamber. Mrs. Abbot bustled over and placed the tray in front of him.

She stood smiling as he dipped his spoon into the stew and blew on it before putting it into his mouth. "You'll be better before you know it if you keep your appetite, Sire."

Simon leaned back in the chair. He tore a chunk of bread and put it in his mouth, chewing slowly. "Tell me about that woman, what was her name…Tip, Tam?"

The smile dropped from her face. Mrs. Abbot scowled. "Do you mean Lady Tig, Sire?"

"Yes, Tig, that was her name."

"I am not the one you should be asking," she said ominously.

"I can tell from your reaction that you are exactly the one I should be speaking to. Tell me."

"Well, I cannot speak for anyone else, Sire, but from the dealings I have had with her, well, let's just say that we are lucky to still be breathing."

"What? Explain that statement."

"She threatened to kill me, Sire, when I would not let her have her way. She has assaulted some of my girls when they were merely trying to help her. Not to mention poor Stephen, Sire. You remember him? Well, she practically castrated him!" Mrs. Abbot's face had turned scarlet red and she was on the verge of tears by the time she had finished.

Simon listened to this diatribe in amazement. This Tig woman seemed to be a terror and yet she was freely walking the halls of the castle.

"Oh, there are other rumors too, Your Highness. We are not the only ones to have been threatened by her."

"Who is she, Mrs. Abbot? How did she come to be here?"

"I'm not really sure, all I have heard is speculation. She has been called a witch and a demon Sire. You should speak to Memron, I believe he can tell you. He has borne the brunt of her anger more than anyone else here," she said cryptically.

The men had finished their equestrian training and had returned to the stables to care for their horses. Tig, Juno, and Griffin rode into the woods to their glade. Tig dismounted, leaving Juno free to feast on the grass. She sat with Griffin, rubbing his massive belly. With Simon's memory of her wiped away, she realized that she might be in a precarious position at the castle.

The facts, on paper, were quite dire. She was the one that had kidnapped him from Sandria and brought him back to Moregane for execution. She had been the cause of him breaking his betrothal to the Duchess of Crissley. She had been the cause of his Military Advisor's execution and the disfigurement of the Duchess. Not many redeeming facts there.

And then there was their relationship. It had not started out easy. Even she had to admit that she had been the cause of many of their arguments and when she really thought about it, she was surprised that they loved each other as deeply as they did.

They were so perfectly suited to one another. Simon, although he was a warrior, was kind and gentle with her and very understanding. She was volatile, easy to anger, quick to strike.

Was there anything about her now that would make him want to be with her again? Without their history could Simon still love her? Tig didn't know. In all honesty, she wanted to grab him by the collar and demand that he love her again. But she couldn't do that. In his current state of mind, he would more than likely throw her into a cell, if not order her execution. She had to come up with a plan on how to deal with Simon and her emotions.

The sun was setting when she mounted Juno and started back to the castle. Night had fallen by the time she arrived at the stables. She took time to rub down Juno and feed her. She entered the castle to find most of its occupants gone for the evening. She went to the kitchen to assemble a cold meal and take it to her tower room to share with Griffin.

Avoidance was her plan. If she avoided Simon, she could conceal her true feelings for him. Perhaps she would slip from his mind until his memory returned.

Simon noticed her absence at supper last night and at breakfast this morning. Again, strangely, he was disappointed. He would speak to Memron to learn more about...Tag? For now, he would meet with John, his secretary.

He spent the entire day in his office. Mrs. Abbot brought lunch for him and John. It was only his rumbling stomach that made him call an end to the day and the paperwork. He entered the common room as supper was being served. He quickly scanned the tables and saw her; she was sitting with her back to the head table. Was she trying to avoid him? He could only guess. At least she was properly attired in a dress.

He had been speaking to the doctor when he next looked up and noticed that she had gone.

Tig's greatest mission that day had been to sneak into Simon's chamber and remove all of her belongings. She took her clothes and toiletries while he was in his office and brought them to her room. She washed and changed for supper successfully without running into Simon. She felt him as soon as he walked into the common room. It took all her effort not to turn to look at him. She knew if she did, the longing in her eyes would give her away and draw his attention to her. She ate as quickly as she could and left immediately when she was done.

CHAPTER 3

Marcus shuffled from one foot to the other. He was in the King's office. He was nervous. He had been summoned here and he didn't know why. He tried to guess at the reason but could not come up with anything.

"Marcus, please, sit down," Simon said. Marcus sat across from Simon. "How are you, Marcus?"

"I am good, Sire."

"You and I have been friends our whole lives. We have known each other since we were boys."

"Yes, Sire."

"I want you to tell me about Lady…" he looked to John.

"Tig, Sire," John said.

"Yes, Lady Tig. What do you know about her, Marcus?" Simon asked.

Marcus made the sign of the cross. "Lady Tig is an outstanding warrior, Sire," he responded. "She trains your knights."

"Why would you do that Marcus," Simon asked.

"Do what?"

"Cross yourself." Simon mimicked Marcus' actions.

"Did I do that? I had not realized. Just habit."

"You do that every time someone's name is mentioned?"

"No, Sire, just Lady Tig." He crossed himself again.

"You just did it again. Tell me why."

"She is cursed, Sire. She told me so herself when you sent me to find her. She is haunted by the children she killed. She speaks to the dead." He crossed himself again.

"She kills children? I find that hard to believe."

"Believe it, Sire. She told me that children have less blood and they die faster. She knew that because she has killed children. She told me there was no salvation for her."

Simon felt a chill run through him. "Has she killed any children lately?"

"No, Sire. Not since you returned with her last year."

"Where was I?"

"We met you in Parna. She was with you at that time."

"Why was I in Parna?"

"I do not know. You should speak to Gilbert, Sire, he is your closest advisor."

"Gilbert? My nephew Gilbert?"

"Yes."

"Where is he?" he asked John.

"He has gone home to visit with his family. He will be returning soon I believe," John replied.

"I will be sure to consult with him when he returns then. Thank you, Marcus."

Marcus quickly left his office. Simon was more confused about Lady Tig. She was a whore but an outstanding warrior. She had killed children and was cursed. She spoke to the dead and assaulted the castle staff. Why on earth was she here? And, since she was here, why was she allowed to roam freely? He would get to the bottom of this story.

Simon was in the library browsing the book shelves. He had a low throbbing headache. He had buried himself in the work required to run a kingdom, work that he was unfamiliar with. There were constant demands, requests, correspondence, meetings…and having just assumed those duties, found them overwhelming. The quiet of the library always calmed him. He had been here for a while and the throbbing in his head was abating. A movement outside caught his attention. It was Tap—he knew that wasn't her name, why couldn't he remember her name? She was walking when Griffin came running up behind her and nipped at her heel. She drew her knife and crouched to face him.

Good Gods, was she going to kill the dog? He truly wondered if that was the case. From what he had heard about her, she was a killer who enjoyed her work.

Griffin jumped back and crouched, growling. Tap sheathed her knife, screamed and started running, Griffin in pursuit. She stopped and turned. Griffin jumped on her. She caught him in a hug, laughing. He licked her face.

Simon smiled. So, she had a tender side—for the dog at least.

Simon was returning to his office, he strode out of a side hallway, almost colliding with someone. He put his hands

out to steady the other person and came face to face with…
was it Tam?

"Sire," she said as she curtsied.

"Lady Tam," he acknowledged her.

"Tig, Sire, my name is Tig."

"Ah, yes, forgive me, Lady Tig." Her eyes were downcast and he took the opportunity to examine her beauty. He brought his hand up, he was going to stroke her cheek, when he stopped. What was he doing? "How has your day been," he asked as he put his hand down and clasped his other hand behind his back.

"Fine. I have finished training the men in the arena."

"Training the men?"

"Yes, I train with them every day."

"What are you training them to do? Dressed like that? What skills do you, a woman, have to teach the men? Should I guess?"

Tig took a deep breath. "I take exception to both the tone of your voice and the implication of your questions, Sire." She glared at him, an edge to her voice.

Her eyes had turned a deep blue, her cheeks flushed and her lips parted. Simon had the urge to grab her and kiss her. How many other men had had that urge and acted on it? He didn't care to guess. "You will answer my questions, Lady Tag. You are bound to respond to your King."

"Well, you are not my King and I am not bound to respond to your insulting questions."

"How do you suppose I am not your King?"

"I was brought here. I am here of my own free will. I am a guest here, not a subject, nor a servant."

"A guest? You are a guest here? Who's guest are you?"

"I am your guest."

"My guest?"

"Yes, Sire."

"Why would I have you here as my guest?"

"Why don't you try to figure that out for yourself," she spat.

She stormed off, leaving Simon in the hallway watching her walk away. She was his guest, she said. His guest. Why would he want her to stay here? From what he had learned about her so far, he should have asked her to leave long ago. He should have been happy to have been rid of her and yet, here she was, apparently at his request.

There could only be one reason that would make sense to him. She must have some sexual expertise that he found appealing; some whore's tricks that not every woman would know. That must be it. That would also explain his reaction to her, why he wanted to touch her. Well, he would find out in time.

Tig was annoyed. She slammed the door to her room and tore the clothes from her body, dropping them on the floor. Simon thought she was a whore, that was obvious. She didn't know how much longer she could bear his insults and allow him to continue with that train of thought. Would he even believe her if she told him the truth? Probably not. She sat on her bed, breathing deeply, trying to rid herself of her annoyance. Something had to break, didn't it? Hopefully it wouldn't be her.

• • •

Tig arrived late for supper. She ate quickly and left as soon as she could. She walked out to the paddock. She had taken an apple for Juno. The sun had set but it was not full dark yet; a glow in the west provided dim lighting. Juno came when Tig called her and gladly ate the apple. Tig scratched behind Juno's ears, looking at the sky. The stars were beginning to shine in the heavens.

"Good evening, Lady Tor," Simon said as he walked up behind her.

She stiffened. "Tig, Sire. My name is Tig."

"Of course, Lady Tig, I apologize."

"Yes, you apologize again, Your Highness," she said testily.

He stood beside her as she stroked Juno's neck. Tig was uncomfortable. She wished he would go away. His actions were so contrary. He seemed to hate her one minute, view her as a whore the next, but he went out of his way tonight to come speak with her.

"It's a lovely night," he said placatingly.

"It's clear enough to see the stars. We don't have the same stars where I come from."

"Where do you come from?"

"Nowhere you have ever heard of."

"I'm not so sure. I am well-travelled, Madam."

"Really? I'm from a lot of places. My last home was in New York City."

"New York City. You have me. I have not heard of it. Do you miss it?"

"Sometimes I do. Usually, no."

Simon pointed at the sky. "That's Tibor, the dragon."

Tig looked up, trying to see what he was pointing at.

Simon moved behind her. He took her hand in his and lifted it, pointing it to the stars. "That's his snout," he started to outline the dragon. "His ears, neck, long back, tail curving around his body."

Tig's body was tingling. She leaned against him. She could smell him. She closed her eyes for a moment enjoying the feel of his body against hers.

"Next to Tibor is Paragon, the ogre," he continued, moving their hands to the right. "His head, his eyes," Simon bent his head to her neck. "His belly, his legs."

"Yes," Tig sighed.

"Up there," Simon whispered, "is the blue planet Aqueous."

"Okay," Tig said.

Tig wasn't listening to him anymore or even looking up at the stars. She was leaning against his body, welcoming the familiar comfort that contact with him brought. It had been only two weeks since his accident and yet she felt as if it had been months since they had been together. She missed him with all her heart.

He nuzzled her neck. "Tor," he gasped.

"For fuck's sake," Tig swore as she pushed him away from her. She spun to face him. "My name is Tig. How hard is that? Tig, Tig, Tig. Try to remember that." She pushed him again, glaring at him. "Tig." She said again before storming off.

She was furious with him. He should know her name. But she was just as angry at herself. She could not give herself to a man with such a low opinion of her, even though she knew he felt their attraction as strongly as she did. From his actions it seemed as if he was willing to explore those feelings despite his obvious dislike of her.

CHAPTER 4

The next day Simon went to the arena to witness exactly what type of training Lady Gam was doing with his men.

He heard them before he entered the arena; the men were shouting. He entered the arena to see the men standing in a circle yelling at what was happening. He pushed his way into the throng. Whatever was happening came to an end. There were disappointed groans and happy "I told you so's". One more push and Simon saw a man standing very still, an arm wrapped around his neck, a knife at this throat. Lady Tab was holding the knife.

Tig pushed the man away from her. "When you figure out where you went wrong, we'll try that again." Her eyes met Simon's. "Sire," she said. The men quickly stood at attention.

Simon nodded at them. "Carry on," he said.

Tig sheathed her knife. "Back to it, fun's over," she said. "Will you be joining us this morning, Sire?"

The men disbursed and returned to their stations to continue training.

"No. I heard the commotion and thought I would come to see what was happening," he lied.

"I was going to come see you this morning Sire," she said. Simon raised his eyebrow at her. "To collect your debt."

"Ah, yes, the five."

"I'll make a deal with you, Sire."

He looked down his nose at her, this was what he had been waiting for. She was going to proposition him, offer herself for more money. "Yes," he said.

"You can keep it and I will give you another five if you tell me my name," she grinned.

"Are you always so insolent?"

"No, that's not my name," she laughed. "Yes, I am always so insolent, and you know what?"

"What?"

"You like it."

Gam turned her back on him, pulled a sword and returned to training with the men.

Simon was sitting in his office. He replayed his exchange with Top in the arena. He smiled. What was this hold that she had on him, and he knew that she had him. Her insolence, her casual attitude toward him was unheard of. He was the King. He could easily have had her punished for turning her back on him and walking away without being dismissed. Rather than calling the guards she presented a puzzle to him that he felt he should solve by himself. He knew how he would like to solve that puzzle too, in his chambers with her naked on his bed…. He coughed and addressed John.

"I want you to speak to the men. Find out how many of them have had relations with Lady Top," he ordered.

"Lady Tig," John corrected him.

"Yes, Lady Tig." Damn it, how come he could not remember her name. He changed the subject. "I want to review the livestock inventory. We need to ensure that we will have enough stock for the winter."

"Yes, Sire."

Simon continued to work long hours in his office, trying to catch up on the paperwork and respond to the demands on his time. He ended most days exhausted with a headache. He would have supper in the common room where Lady whatever-her-name-is would not be and that would add a layer of annoyance to his exhaustion. Then he would retire to his chambers and go directly to bed.

He wanted to continue his investigation of Lady Tada but his days were long and he did not have time to spare for things that were not urgent.

Later that month, after having found an hour or two available, he had summoned Memron to his office. Memron stood before the King. He shuffled from one foot to the other, his fingers twisting in his robe. The King and he were not on the best of terms and mostly agreed to avoid each other. The fact that he had been summoned to meet with the King made him uneasy.

"I have been told a number of times that I should speak to you, Memron, about Lady…" he looked at John.

"Lady Tig."

"Yes, Lady Tig, Memron. Where is she from?"

"I conjured her from another dimension on your brother's orders, Sire."

Simon's head jerked back at his words, a look of confusion quickly covering his face. "How long has she been here?"

"The first time—" Memron began.

"The first time? She has been here more than once?"

"Yes, Sire. The first time she was here for less than a year. The second and last time I brought her here was a little over four years ago."

Simon jerked at his words again. Memron watched as Simon digested this information. Memron realized then that the rumors of the King's memory loss were true. He didn't know who Tig was. He didn't know the hand that Memron had played in bringing her here.

"Who is she, Memron?"

"She is a killer, Sire."

"Why would Cameron order you to bring a killer to Moregane? Couldn't you fill that request with one of the knights or perhaps a mercenary?"

Memron thought fast. He had to respond truthfully and in the most general terms. He needed to ensure that his hand in any wrongdoing was reduced to minimal involvement. He had been ordered to find someone to kidnap Simon in Sandria and bring him back to Vestry for execution by Cameron. That was how he found Tig and brought her here with the knowledge that she would have a hand in Simon's execution. He wanted to come out of this interview looking as innocent as possible. "King Cameron rejected all local talent. He wanted someone unknown to our country."

"And, so, she performed her task and she was sent away?"

"Yes, Sire. She asked that she be sent home."

"Why was she brought back?"

"Again, Sire, circumstances dictated that she be recalled to complete a task that only she was capable of executing."

How do you tell your King that Sophie, his former betrothed, had captured him and was going to execute him while, unknown to all, his former military advisor was involved with Sophie and had concocted this plan to capture Tig and kill her. There was no way to tell him that and, again, admit his involvement in bringing Tig back to Vestry, casting suspicion on his possible involvement in that plan.

"And you are on friendly terms with her?"

"No, Sire, the last time I brought her here she almost killed me. If the guards had not been so quick to respond I could very well be dead. We are certainly not friends. I believe she hates the sight of me."

Simon dismissed Memron. Nothing made sense to him. He now confirmed that she was a killer, and a very good one from the sound of it, but why was she still here? Why had she been allowed to stay?

CHAPTER 5

Lady Tic was avoiding him, Simon knew it. He hadn't seen her for weeks. He would catch glimpses of her through the window of his office or as he was walking through the halls of the castle. In the moments when he was not busy with running the castle and the kingdom, he would think back to their night looking at the stars. He would get a strange yearning in the pit of his stomach that he would forcefully have to quash.

Thinking back to that night, Tig regretted every moment of it. She was sure Simon still didn't know her name. She regretted her weakness when she had leaned against him. It had seemed at the time that the real Simon was with her and she missed him, she craved him. If he had not called her "Tor" and pulled her back to reality, she would have allowed him more than a kiss on the neck. And then she had flirted with him the very next day. She had to stick to her plan to avoid him until he regained his memory, she felt her position here was still very precarious.

Simon was in the stable speaking to the head groom,

discussing which mares would be bred in the spring when a page came running toward him.

"Sire," he said, breathlessly.

"Yes," Simon responded.

"The Earl of Greenbrook wishes an audience. He is here from Fallsteppe, he and his son."

"Fallsteppe? He has travelled a great distance. I will meet with him in my office. See that he is escorted there."

"Yes, Sire." The page bowed and ran back to the castle.

Twenty minutes later Simon entered his office.

"Your Highness," the Earl stood and bowed.

"Sir, I understand you are here from Fallsteppe. Are you passing through?"

"No, no. I am here to beg a favor, Sire."

"I'm not sure what I can do for you but, please, proceed."

"When I heard the Demon was training your soldiers, I had to bring my son and ask that he be allowed to pledge his fealty to you in exchange for his training."

"The Demon?" Simon looked at John. John shrugged his shoulders.

"Yes, I had the privilege of seeing her in the arena in Skree three times. I was left breathless. You are lucky indeed to have her in your employ."

"You saw her in the arena in Skree?" Simon was shocked at this. "What did you see?"

"Surely, you must know of her reputation. You must have seen her yourself."

"Indulge me, Sir."

"The first time I saw her, she dispatched three armed

men in a matter of minutes and not a scratch on her!" The Earl was excited in reliving this moment. "The second time it was five men. The last time she slew a giant as tall as a tree, truly!" He continued on, speaking quickly in his excitement. "Each time she slew her opponents with speed and ease. Those men didn't stand a chance against her. If she is teaching your men, it would be an honor for my son to be allowed to train with her."

Simon turned his back on the Earl, taking a moment to digest this new information. Tid was a famous fighter in the arena of Skree, a famous killer.

"I think perhaps you may be mistaken but, nonetheless, let's discuss training your son with Lady..." he looked at John.

"Lady Tig."

"Yes, Lady Tig." Simon called a page. "Bring Lady Tig to me."

"Yes, Sire," the boy bowed and left Simon's office.

"A drink while we wait?" he asked the Earl.

"Yes, I would enjoy that."

Simon poured two glasses of whiskey. They discussed the Earl's journey while waiting for Tig. Fifteen minutes later she strode into his office.

She noted the Earl when she entered Simon's office, but her eyes went to Simon. "Sire," she said.

"Lady...Madam, I would like you to meet the Earl of Greenbrook. He has travelled from Fallsteppe to ask a favor," Simon said. "Sir," he addressed the Earl.

The Earl put down his glass and rose. He walked toward Tig and put his hand out. "Madam, I am an admirer," he said as he took her hand and raised it to his lips.

Tig pulled her hand away. "I'm afraid we have not met before, Sir."

"No, we have never met, but I know who you are. I have had the privilege—no, the honor, of witnessing your skills in the arena in Skree."

Simon was surprised by her reaction. Tig stood taller, her nostrils flared, and she skewered him with a glare of blazing hot anger. "What is the favor you wish," she ground out between clenched teeth.

Simon responded, "He would like you to train his son. In return, his son will swear fealty to me."

"I will assess him to see if he is acceptable." She motioned for the page who had summoned her to Simon's office. "Take the Earl and his son to the arena," she instructed.

The page addressed the Earl, "If you will follow me, sir." He exited the room with the Earl following him.

Tig turned to Simon. "A word, Sire," she said.

Simon nodded his head.

"Don't you ever do that to me again," she spat out. She was still angry; her eyes were blazing at him.

"Is that an order, Madam? You seem to be forgetting yourself. I do not take orders from you, or anyone. Anyway, I thought you would enjoy meeting someone who was pleased with your performance."

"My performance," Tig yelled. "I was fighting for my life each and every time. Do not mistake that what I was doing as a theatrical performance. Lives were lost."

"At your hand. You seem to have done very well for yourself."

"Fuck you," she spat, glaring at him. Her chin was jutted out, her eyes narrowed, her body tense.

He had every right as King to slap her for those words, but he didn't want to and he didn't know why. He could have had her put in a cell for one month for her conduct, but he wasn't going to. Simon felt threatened but he also recognized her restraint in not launching herself at him. It seemed Lady Whoever had a temper. He would have to remember that.

"Yes, fuck me, whatever that is. You will watch your tongue, Lady Tif, lest you lose it," he warned. He was angry now too. He had the unexplainable urge to take her in his arms, to try to calm her with kisses and sweet words. Instead, he said, "To the arena, then."

They walked the halls to the arena, Tig striding angrily ahead of him.

The Earl and his son were waiting for them. "Lady Tig, my son Taryn," the Earl said.

Tig nodded her head and then indicated that he was to enter the arena with her. She pointed to a spot. Taryn took his place as Tig sized him up. He was a big beefy boy. He would be fat in five years' time. She strongly suspected that, rather than a fighter, he was a bully who picked on those smaller and weaker than him.

She stood in front of him. "So, you're a fighter?"

"Yes, Madam, a good fighter."

"Let's see what you have then," she said.

Taryn looked at her in confusion, uncertain if he was to fight her. He looked to his father.

"What are you looking at? I said, let's see what you have," she demanded.

Still, he stood there, unsure of what to do.

"Do you need incentive?" Tig asked as she walked up to him and slapped his face. Taryn's head rocked back.

The men had gathered to watch. They had seen this before. Some of them had been in Taryn's place.

Taryn, stood his ground. Tig whipped out a hand and slapped him again.

"Are you going to just stand there? I can do this all day." She slapped him again. "Come on, fight!"

"I'm not going to fight a woma—"

Tig punched him in the stomach and he doubled over. "You're not going to fight a what?" She lashed out with an upper cut to the chin, forcing him to stand up straight. She stood back, easily within Taryn's reach, waiting for his first move. She watched his eyes. There was concern written on his face. He was wondering if he could fight her and win.

"Just as I thought," she said as she turned to walk toward the Earl. "Take him back to his mother, there is no place for him here."

Taryn roared and barreled toward Tig.

Tig's back was turned to Taryn, but she was expecting this. She spun quickly and stuck her foot out. He tripped and fell into the dirt. The men were laughing. Taryn was humiliated. He sprung up and ran at Tig again.

"Taryn," his father yelled.

Taryn was past hearing. He was focused with lethal intensity on Tig. Tig knew what he was thinking, that she could not treat him like this, after all, he was Taryn, son of the Earl of Greenbrook!

Tig waited for him.

Taryn was within Tig's reach when he put his arms out to grab her. Grab her and kill her. He sped toward her, Tig took half a step to the right, reached out, grabbed one of his arms and spun him around. She pulled him up against her, a sai sword at his neck. Taryn stood still.

Tig leaned toward him and whispered in his ear. "Make no mistake, Taryn, I should kill you. I don't care that your father is standing there. You are a coward and a bully. I only train men." She pulled her sword away from his neck, sheathed it, and walked away.

"Lady Tig," the Earl called after her.

She ignored him and left the arena.

She was still furious at Simon. Normally, he would have dealt with these matters and had applicants prescreened before she met them. She was working hard to rid herself of The Demon. She had put in intensive self-examination to reconcile herself to the fact that she was "The Demon" and that she had killed for sport, although, in fact, it was survival.

The old Simon knew this and was working with her in trying to rid herself of The Demon. This Simon did not know, did not care, and was unaware of how distressing this was to her.

She went to the stable, saddled Juno and left the castle with Griffin close behind.

CHAPTER 6

Tig continued to avoid Simon.

Simon suspected she was still angry with him, but he did not make an effort to see her. Perhaps this distance between them was best. She aroused feelings in him that he could not explain and that, quite frankly, troubled him. Why he would feel such tender feelings toward a killer was beyond him. Granted, she was a beautiful woman, but she seemed to be a bit of a powder keg.

He entered his office. John was waiting for him.

"Sire, I have completed my interviews with the men," he said.

Simon looked at him quizzically.

"You asked that I find out how many men Lady Tig had 'entertained'."

"Ah, yes." He had asked John to investigate quite some time ago. If Simon was busy, John was doubly so, having to carry out his instructions. "What did you find out?" Simon asked as he sat behind his desk, prepared to hear about her wantonness and her conquests.

"None of the men have enjoyed her company."

"None of the men. Really."

"Yes, Sire. It is common knowledge that she is your woman, Sire."

"What?"

"The men are all of the opinion that you are the only one who has—"

"Surely, those are rumors."

"No, Sire, I don't believe they are."

"Are the men that convincing?"

"Sire, I have seen it with my own eyes."

"You have?"

"Yes, Sire. You seem to have had deep feelings for her. When you returned from Parna with her, she spent her nights in your chamber, Sire."

"I don't find this amusing, John."

"I am telling the truth."

This was unbelievable. Lady Tib was his woman? She spent her nights in his chamber? Not possible!

Simon rose, left his office and strode down the hall to his chamber. He stood in the room. There were two chests. He opened one; his clothes were there. He went to the next chest; it was empty. He walked to the wardrobe and opened one door; his clothes hung there. He opened the other door; it was empty. Next, he went to the chest of drawers. He opened the drawers, half of them were full of his clothing. The other half of the drawers were empty. He noticed for the first time that his toiletries were neatly arranged on the top of the chest of drawers. But they were only on one side.

Could it be true? Could Lady Gab be his woman? Had she shared his chamber? It would appear so. He couldn't seem to wrap his mind around the thought of them together, though that would explain his tender feelings for her. Maybe that was why he always wanted to touch her when she was near. Still, though, he could have any woman—and he had had many—who weren't killers. As a matter of fact, being a killer was definitely not an attribute that he sought in his women.

He had a full agenda of items that needed tending to. He would deal with this later.

He left his chamber and returned to his office.

Supper was over, the day was nearing an end. He called a guard. "Find Lady Tad. Take her to my chambers. She is to wait for me there," he ordered.

The guard bowed. "Yes, Sire."

Simon lingered in the common room. He shared a drink with his men before finally rising. He was looking forward to the evening ahead.

Tig stood in Simon's chamber. She didn't know what this was about. She didn't know where Simon was. She was starting to get annoyed that he had her brought here and was making her wait.

The door opened and Simon walked in. Pushing the door closed behind him, he addressed Tig. "You may disrobe," he said as he passed her and walked across the room.

He took his jacket off and tossed it on a chair. He turned toward her. He unbuttoned the sleeves of his shirt, then the buttons at his neck. He pulled his shirt off. He stood still looking at her.

Tig was watching him. "What is this about," she asked.

"I have been informed that we—you and I—are a couple. I find it hard to believe. So, I will find out whether those rumors are true. You are still dressed."

"Yes, I am."

"I told you to disrobe."

"You can't tell me what to do. I have no intention of taking my clothes off."

"Is that how it is between us? You are the virginal maiden or the cold cunt and you make me beg you for affection?" He walked toward her. "If that's so, that is not how it is now. Those days are over."

Simon could have plunged a knife into her chest and hurt her less. She knew he didn't fully understand their relationship, she realized she should forgive him for his ignorance but, easier said than done.

He stood before her; his chest bare. He unbuttoned his pants; they slid down his hips.

"That is not how it was," Tig said. She couldn't seem to think clearly. "I'm not…"

Simon grabbed her arm, glaring at her. "How was it then? Do you prefer to have your skirts over your head?"

He pushed her down on the bed. He bent and grabbed the hem of her skirt, pulling it up over her knees. Tig put both hands on her skirt, stopping him and giving her a moment to breathe. He was so close; he was almost naked. It would be so easy for her to let him have his way and relieve the yearning she felt, but, again, easier said than done. He wanted her but he still thought of her as his whore.

"Stop," she said. She looked into his eyes. There was passion there, but no tender feelings. "Please."

"This is going to happen, Lady Tod. Is it romance you want?" He put his hands on the back of her head and bent toward her, his lips lightly brushing hers. She felt the electricity in that kiss. She knew that he did too. The look of shock on his face let her know that. For a moment she saw a glimpse of desire flash through his eyes before being replaced with pure lust. He leaned in again with a more demanding kiss.

Tig pushed him away, tearing her lips from his. God, she wanted him. She could have him. She could let him take her and she would enjoy it. But not like this. There was no emotion there. He didn't even seem to like her. She was not going to be his toy, to be used and discarded when he tired of her.

Simon took her hands in his and pushed them down. He pushed her back on the bed and lay on top of her, kissing her again, grinding his hips into her.

"Stop. Not like this," Tig smiled at him, this is enough of that she thought. "I'll show you," she said as she wrapped her arms around him and rolled on top of him. She rested her hands on his chest, looking down at him. She stroked his cheek, trailing her hand down to his neck. She gripped his neck, watching him. She exerted more pressure. He closed his eyes and passed out.

"You asshole," she said as she slapped him.

She stood, arranged her skirt and turned toward the door.

"Tig," Simon sighed.

She turned toward him, hopeful that he was calling to her, knew that she was there, but no, he was still out. She leaned over and kissed him. She picked up a throw and covered him before leaving, closing the door quietly behind her.

Simon slept deeply and dreamed. He saw images of a woman walking out of a lake, water dripping from her body. She stood before him. He felt desire course through his body. Then he saw Tig, a knife pressed against his throat.

"I could kill you right now," she said.

"A threat on the King's life is a death sentence," he responded.

"If I die, I'm taking you with me," she said.

He woke with a start, looking wildly around the room. Was Tib in his room? Was she going to kill him? No. He was quite alone. In his bed. His pants on. Covered with a throw.

He thought back to last night…he'd had Tin in his room. He had unbelievably learned that she was his woman and had planned on proving that rumor. She had been on top of him…. And that was all that he remembered.

Later that day he met her in the hall; she nodded at him and continued to walk past him. He reached out and grabbed her arm.

"Say it," he said.

He looked at her with amusement in his eyes. "Sire," she exhaled.

Simon seemed to be frozen, looking at her. Had that

just happened? It seemed as if he had been watching himself and Tic from afar. "Yes, Sire?" she asked, snapping him back to reality.

He shook his head and focused on her. "It seems we were interrupted last night."

"No, Sire, you fell asleep. You were quite tired."

"I was not tired, Madam."

"You were. I believe your exact words were 'I'm exhausted. I'm too tired to rape you tonight', and then you fell asleep."

He felt shame burn his cheeks. He released her arm and walked away.

CHAPTER 7

Tig continued her routine, training with the men and avoiding Simon. Time was passing and still there was no indication that he was regaining his memory. Sometimes when she saw him, he would look at her as if he was trying to figure something out and that gave her hope. Other times he would look at her as if she didn't exist, or worse, like she was dirt beneath his feet. Those were the times that she wondered why she was still here, what she was waiting for.

The episode in his chamber was not repeated. Tig was grateful and disappointed at the same time. She knew that if his efforts to take her were to continue she would not have been able to resist him for long. She yearned for his touch—Simon's touch, not this man's touch. But this man looked just like Simon, he sounded like him and smelled like him too. The problem was that she was nothing more than an exercise to this man. She didn't know if she could be satisfied with that type of arrangement with this man. It was better for her to avoid him and not face that dilemma.

Simon continued to have dreams of the mystery woman. They had advanced to the point where he was having sex with her—wild, passionate sex. He would often wake with an erection that had to be dealt with before he could leave his chamber. Even so, as he held his cock in his hand, he would picture her and remember his dreams. He would come hard every time, thinking that if she was real, he had been a fool to let her go.

It was now three months since Simon had lost his memory. Tig was passing through the common room.

Mrs. Abbot was speaking to a young maid. "Open the queen's room. Make sure that you clean it well. That's where the Duchess will be staying."

Tig jerked to a stop. She turned toward Mrs. Abbott. "What did you just say?" she demanded.

Mrs. Abbott paled. "Nothing, Lady Tig. I didn't say anything."

"Yes, you did. What about the queen's room? Who is coming?"

"The queen's room must be opened and cleaned. The Duchess of Crissley is coming."

"Why is she coming here?"

"The King has invited her."

"When will she arrive?"

"We are expecting her within the week."

Tig stormed into Simon's office. She stopped in front of his desk. He glanced up from his paperwork.

"If you wish to speak to me, you must follow procedure—" Simon said, an edge of irritation in his voice.

"Why did you invite Sophie to come here," Tig spat out.

"You know the Duchess?" Simon asked, his eyebrows

raised. He leaned back in his chair, observing her. She was angry. Her face was flushed, her eyes flashing, her body tense.

"Oh, I know her all right. Why did you invite her here," Tig repeated.

"If you know her, you must know that we are betrothed," he responded coolly. "I wish to spend time with her. We should begin planning our wedding."

"You can't be serious."

"I am serious, and I fail to see why any of this is your concern."

"You know why it's my concern Simon."

"First of all, do not address me by my name. You are to address me as—"

"Sire or Your Highness. I know that, Simon," she said, deliberately trying to annoy him. She was angry and she wanted him to be angry too, even if it was at her.

It worked. "I don't know why this is your concern."

"You do too Simon. I won't allow you to bring her here."

"YOU won't allow me?"

"That's right. You can't. I won't let you."

"I remind you that you have no say in what I do, Lady Tif."

"MY FUCKING NAME IS TIG," she screamed at him.

"I DON'T CARE WHAT YOUR NAME IS. DUCHESS CRISSLEY IS COMING HERE AND I DON'T GIVE A DAMN WHAT YOU THINK."

"Fine," Tig spat. "When you finally remember

everything, you are going to recall this conversation and you are going to feel like the enormous ass that you are!"

His hand shot out, grabbing her arm and pulling her toward him. He pushed his face up to hers. "Leave now." He glared at her before releasing her and pushing her away from him.

"Don't worry, Simon. I'm going." Tig turned and left, slamming the door to his office.

Tig entered her tower room and forcefully slammed the door behind her. She had to think. She paced the small confines of her room, a kaleidoscope of images running through her head.

Being forced to the ground by the weight of a net. Being knocked unconscious by a blow to her head. Awakening in a cage on the back of a wagon with Sophie's venomous voice telling her that she would pray for death. Being sold into slavery. Being tortured and then addicted into compliance. Being forced to kill for sport in order to survive. Seeing Sophie gloating at her, hearing her voice again and again saying "You will pray for death".

She slammed her fists over her ears and fell onto her bed. More images… Simon killing Clarence for his part in this plan. Her cutting Sophie's face, disfiguring her for life.

She could not say here any longer. When Sophie arrived she would see to it that Tig were punished for her disfigurement. Simon would promise it to his love, not remembering what had happened. She had to leave and she had to do it today or possibly lose her life.

In the early hours of the morning while the castle slept, Tig crept down the stairs from her tower room. She went to the kitchen and packed some food, then stole out to the paddock. She saddled Juno and walked her out of the courtyard, Griffin at her heel. On the plain, she mounted Juno and urged her to a run, away from the castle, away from Moregane, and away from Simon.

Four days later the Duchess of Crissley arrived. Simon met the carriage as it arrived in the courtyard. He was glad to have Sophie here. He hoped that with her here his erotic dreams would come to an end.

He put his hand into the carriage. Sophie gripped his fingers and stepped out. Simon was surprised to see that her face was covered by a heavy veil. He moved to lift it and see her face. Her other hand came up to stop him. "Once we are inside Simon, please," she said.

He bowed to her request and preceded her into the castle, to a sitting room. Sophie followed him in. She walked to a table and removed her gloves. A maid came in with a tray of cakes and tea. Sophie turned her back on the maid and Simon, lifted the veil and draped it on her shoulders. The maid left. Sophie turned to Simon, waiting for his reaction.

Simon looked at her face and gasped. There was a scar on the right side of her face running from the corner of her eye to the corner of her mouth. It was angry, red, and puckered. It pulled the corner of her eye down and pulled the right side of her mouth up into an evil sneer.

Sophie began crying and hurled herself into his arms.

"You don't love me anymore. I know you can't, but I wanted to see you one last time."

He held her in his arms. "Sophie," he cooed to her, "you are still the Sophie I have always known. You haven't changed." He rubbed her back as he comforted her.

She pulled away from him and looked into his eyes. "Do you mean that Simon?"

"Of course, I do," he reassured her. He pulled her back into his arms.

She clung to him, crying again. When she had calmed herself, she pulled away from him and sat down.

"What happened, Sophie?" Simon asked gently.

"Your whore Tig happened, Simon."

Simon was immediately angry. "Tell me," he ordered.

"When I left last time, she followed me back to Freecourt and attacked me. She knew that you loved me more. I begged her not to hurt me, but she didn't listen. She cut my face. She said she would make sure you would never look at me again. She said she would be your queen and that you couldn't love me because I would be a monster."

Simon leapt up and went to the doors. He flung them open. "Guards," he called. Two guards ran to him. "Find Tig and bring her to me immediately. NOW." He was furious. She had gone too far. She would pay for this. He would make sure of it.

He returned to Sophie. "She will pay for this, Sophie. She will not go unpunished."

Sophie smiled. That was exactly what she had planned.

When she received Simon's letter that explained his situation and invited her to come to Moregane to plan their wedding, she had leapt at the opportunity.

Tig would suffer at her hands yet again. Simon had responded exactly the way she had hoped he would. Tig would be punished and she, Sophie, would be Simon's queen and there would be nothing that Tig could do but suffer. She would regret the day she ever met Sophie. Sophie would see to it. She thought perhaps the loss of a limb might be a good way to start. She would make it happen. But which limb? An arm? A leg?

Decisions, decisions, she sighed to herself.

An hour later the guards returned to the sitting room. They reported that Lady Tig was missing and seemed to have been gone for days. They added that one of the horses and the dog, Griffin, were gone as well. Simon ordered a small party to find her and to bring her back to the castle. He assured Sophie that Tig would not get away with the attack on the Duchess.

Sophie basked in Simon's determination to exact revenge, in his steadfast belief in her words. Sophie still had nightmares about that day. Simon had returned to Freecourt and was waiting for her in the drawing room, she was certain, to beg her forgiveness, wanting to reinstate their betrothal. Instead, she had entered the drawing room to find Simon standing beside Clarence, her co-conspirator in dealing with Tig, and Tig. Simon had plunged a knife into Clarence's throat. Clarence died in front of her and then Tig had pinned her to the floor. She had begged

Simon to help her but he was deaf to her pleas and Tig had cut her face, disfiguring her for life.

Oh yes, Simon's accident had been for the best, she couldn't have hoped for anything better.

CHAPTER 8

Tig rode hard for a week, pushing herself, Juno, and Griffin to their limits. She hoped that she would have at least two days head start on her escape. She rode the main road. If Simon sent trackers after her she hoped that her tracks would be covered by other travelers on the road. Although her intent was to remain anonymous, she knew that travelling with Griffin would make her stand out and she was not prepared to send him home or abandon him.

There were many travelers on the road. Tig rode past them all without stopping to chat. She would make brief eye contact or nod in passing, but no words were spoken. She avoided all towns and villages, skirting them before returning to the road.

She rode from sunrise to dusk when she would ride off the road, making camp in a grassy area for Juno to graze. Griffin would find his own supper and then they would bed down for the night. Tig slept soundly from exhaustion and in the knowledge that Griffin would alert her if anyone were to approach their camp. She was up before dawn to do her exercises, eat a small breakfast, and then saddle Juno to continue their journey to nowhere.

By her sixth week on the road, they were travelling at a more leisurely pace. The geography of the land had changed from forest to plains to rolling hills. She woke to a beautiful day; the sun warmed her as she rode. They were at a deserted stretch of road when she veered off onto a cart track. She followed it for the day, meeting no one, but passing several cottages. The sun was starting to set, she hadn't passed a cottage for several hours. The track petered out and they crested one more hill. There before them was a large blue lake with a stand of trees nearby.

Tig felt a sense of contentment wash over her. She steered Juno toward the trees. It was time to rest.

The party Simon had sent after Tig returned a week later. They had found no trace of her. She had travelled the main road, her tracks lost among those of all the other travelers. They did meet some people who had seen her riding but they said it had been days ago, that they did not speak with her, and they had no idea where she was headed.

On the one hand, Simon was angry that she had escaped but, on the other hand, he felt relieved that such a dangerous person was no longer living in the castle. She had presented a large problem to him in another area. She was apparently his woman but they had no relationship now. He had brought Sophie to Moregane to plan their wedding and her presence would have made things awkward, he felt, especially given their last exchange before she left. But now she was gone and he didn't have to worry about her interference with his marriage plans.

Simon was in his office, working with John. Sophie entered, Mrs. Abbot at her side. "Simon," Sophie called.

Simon stopped what he was doing, giving his full

attention to Sophie. "Mrs. Abbot and I are planning our wedding feast. I thought it would be wonderful to have game hens as the main course with assorted vegetables, maybe some soup to start. What do you think?"

Simon smiled at Sophie. "I think that whatever you and Mrs. Abbot decide upon will be more than adequate."

"I want something 'more than adequate' for our wedding, Simon," Sophie said. "Don't forget that some of our guests will be travelling from some distance. I want the news of our wedding to travel through all the countries. Our wedding should be the one that everyone wants to emulate, don't you agree?"

Simon stood and walked to her. "The prize at my wedding will be you, Sophie. No one else will be able to emulate that." He bent to kiss her. Sophie turned her head, his lips landing on her cheek.

"You are so sweet, Simon, but I do want your input on matters. It will be your day as much as mine."

"I know that, but the details are no matter to me as long as, by the end of the day, you are my wife."

Sophie looked at Mrs. Abbot. "Men! They have no sense of pageantry. Well, come on then, we still need to discuss dessert and our cake." She turned and left, taking Mrs. Abbot with her.

Simon breathed a sigh of relief. As far as he was concerned, all they needed was a priest, no guests, no feast, no celebration. Sophie wanted a grand event, she wanted to decorate the courtyard and the road from the forest to the castle. Gods, could one even decorate a road? Apparently, it was possible, and Sophie intended to have it done.

"I'm done today," he said to John, rising from his desk and leaving his office.

He walked aimlessly through the halls of the castle, at last finding himself in the library. He stood looking out the window, recalling the time he had seen Griffin and Lady Tot. He thought she was going to kill the dog for nipping at her, but she hadn't. He smiled at the thought.

Suddenly Sophie was standing at his side. "What are you smiling at?" she asked, a smile on her lips.

"Nothing," he said. "Just a happy memory."

"You're thinking of her, aren't you?" Acid dripped from her words.

"Who?"

"You know who. Tig! You're thinking of her!"

"Why would I be thinking of her when I have you right here?" He reached for Sophie, intending to pull her into his arms.

She avoided his embrace. "Why would you have anything to do with a woman like that in the first place? I still can't fathom it and yet you did. I was lucky to survive her attack on me. She almost killed me. Perhaps you would prefer to marry her!"

"I'm not going to marry her, Sophie," he said placatingly. "You are here. She is not."

"And if she were, what then?"

"Well, she's not. I don't expect either of us will ever see her again. There's no need to think of it further."

"Yes, Simon. There is no need to think of Tig. Ever again."

"Matter settled." He smiled at her and reached for her

again. She allowed him to pull her into an embrace, but she stood stiffly against him. He bent down to kiss her and she permitted a brief brush of his lips on hers. He looked into her eyes and bent again, intending to claim her lips.

She pushed herself out of his arms. "Really, Simon, what if someone saw us?"

"Let them see us," he said. "We are going to be husband and wife in a short time. I'm sure people are well aware of what happens between a woman and a man. It would come as no shock to them."

"We will be more than husband and wife," she retorted. "We will be their King and Queen. We must conduct ourselves accordingly, not like animals rutting in the mud."

Simon looked at her coldly. "Is that how you truly feel, Sophie? That a touch from me is like a touch from an animal?"

"No. No, that was not what I was implying, Simon." She put her hand on his arm. "I enjoy your touch, but in the right place and at the right time." She smiled at him. "I look forward to being in the right place at the right time with you." She looked down, her cheeks flushing.

"We could make it the right place and time now Sophie," he said.

"In the middle of the afternoon," she laughed. "We're not married yet, Simon. You are funny." She shook her head and left the library.

That night Simon had another of those dreams. The mystery woman sat naked before him; her legs opened. She reached up and grabbed his shirt, pulling his lips to hers. He entered her and she groaned in response. He could feel her warmth surrounding his cock, her hands caressing him. He could hear her groans of pleasure. He could almost see her face, but it was in shadow. He woke slowly, the sensations still running through his body, his cock standing at attention. He groaned in frustration. He gripped his cock, closing his eyes, picturing her body, remembering her groans. When he came, he released the breath he had been holding. Who was she?

CHAPTER 9

Tig woke with a start, then relaxed when she remembered where she was. She stretched beneath her blanket and pulled it over her face. She heard Griffin rise and walk over to her. She heard him snuffle at the blanket where her face was. "Don't make me get up, Grif," she said.

Griffin whined and pawed at the blanket.

"Don't do it, Grif," she warned.

Griffin barked a short sharp bark.

Suddenly, Tig shot her arms up, holding the blanket. She threw it over Griffin's head and put him in a choke hold. "Got ya," she laughed.

They wrestled, Griffin trying to get away, Tig holding on, trying to turn him over onto his back. In the end Griffin won, pulling out of her grip. She got up and began her yoga stretches. Once she was done, she rigged a branch, a line, and a hook, fashioning a bobber from a dried twig. She stuck the branch into the ground and went for a run. By the time she returned she had a pike on the line.

She pulled the fish out of the water, killed it, then slit it open pulling the guts out and throwing them to Griffin who eagerly gobbled them up. She started a small fire, tied the fish to another stick, and cooked it over the fire. It was delicious.

Done with breakfast, she pulled out her sais and began

her exercises. When she was done with those, she pulled out her throwing stars and did those exercises. Practice made perfect; her stars hit the target she had selected every time. Lastly, she pulled out her sword and went through those exercises.

She was sweating when she was done. She stripped out of her clothes and ran into the lake, diving under the cool water. When she came up, she found Griffin in the water with her. She splashed him. He opened his mouth to catch the waves of water she pushed toward him. She laughed as she walked out of the water. She sat in the sun on a large rock on the shore, drying herself off. It was warm; she had had a good work out. She lay back, looking at the sky, watching an eagle glide above her.

She must have fallen asleep. She was curled up on her side when someone brushed the hair from her forehead. She knew who it was. She opened her eyes. Simon was leaning over her, smiling. She smiled back at him. "There you are," he said.

"It's about time," she mumbled.

"What do you mean?" he asked.

"You've been gone a long time, Simon. I'd given up hope of seeing you again."

"I've been here all along, Tig."

"No, you haven't."

"Yes, I have."

"And now you are going to marry Sophie."

"Yes, I am."

"Why are you doing this?"

"Because she is a lady and you are a whore." He glared at her.

She woke with a start, sitting up looking for Simon, but, of course, he was not there.

"You can't do that," she screamed at no one. "I won't let you do that to me. Stay away from me."

Griffin was at her side in a second. He butted his head into her chest.

"It's okay, Grif. I'm fine. Or I will be. I will be fine, just watch me. I will be fine."

She got up and got dressed. The day had slipped away from her. Time to catch another fish for supper.

Simon and Sophie were walking the ramparts after supper. She held onto his arm with both of her hands, leaning against him. They stopped, looking across the plain to the forest beyond.

"We are going to have trees planted along the road," Sophie said. "In between the trees will be huge vases filled with white roses. We should get a string quartet to play something romantic as our guests arrive. Don't you think that's a good idea?" She looked up at him.

Simon looked toward the road, trying to picture the vision Sophie proposed. There was a movement to the left, just within his eyesight. He quickly turned his head. There she was, on a horse. Through a haze he watched her. She was riding away from the castle. He was about to call out to her when she jumped off the horse and started running after it.

"Simon, what do you think of the string quartet," he heard Sophie ask again.

The woman, caught up to the horse, grabbed the saddle and vaulted onto the horse in a fluid motion. He sucked in his breath.

"Simon," Sophie whined.

She pulled her legs up and stood on the horse's hind quarters, her arms spread, her hair flying in the wind.

"Simon, where are you? Don't ignore me!"

The haze disappeared. So did the woman. "I'm sorry Sophie, I thought I saw something."

"Really, you are so easily distracted these days. What do you think of the string quartet?"

"Whatever you want is what we'll get."

"So, we're agreed?"

"Yes, we are."

She squealed, squeezing his arm. "Our wedding will be a topic of conversation for years! Thank you, Simon." She leaned into him, stood on tiptoe, and kissed his cheek.

Simon turned to her and took her in his arms. Sophie stiffened as he pressed his lips to hers. Sophie tried to pull away, but Simon held her firmly in his arms. He kissed her again, trying to get a response from her.

She pushed at his chest again; Simon released her. She slapped his face. "What do you think I am? We are not married yet, Simon. How dare you!" She was furious.

"You will not slap me again, Sophie," he snapped at her. "What do I think you are? I thought you were the woman I would share the rest of my life with. If you cannot bear my touch now, what will happen after we are married?"

"Don't worry, Simon, I will give you an heir. That much I promise you," she snapped back at him.

"And after you give me an heir?"

"What do you mean?"

"After you give me an heir, will we still share a bed?"

"We don't have to share a bed to conceive a child, Simon. You will visit me in my chamber until the deed is done."

"The deed?"

"Yes."

Simon blew out a breath. Is this the woman he wanted to share his life with? He was beginning to doubt that that would be a wise decision. "Let's go inside, Sophie," he said as he turned back in the direction they had come from.

Sophie smiled. "Yes. I'm glad that you are seeing things my way."

"I didn't say that, Sophie, not at all."

Sophie faltered and then caught herself. "You will, Simon." She glanced at him slyly. "If you truly love me, you will."

That night the mystery woman was back. This time, though, the dream was different. He was surrounded by warmth and comfort. She sat on his lap, leaning against him, his hand resting on her thigh. He was filled with peace and contentment.

CHAPTER 10

By the third day of solitude at the lake, Tig was getting tired of herself and fish. She was unused to idleness. She had greatly improved her fishing skills and worked on her hunting and trapping skills with her limited resources. She had to get on with her life. She couldn't stay here forever.

On the fifth day she packed her belongings, saddled Juno, and went back down the trail she had followed to the main road. She turned left and rode farther away from Moregane and Simon with no destination in mind.

As she rode, she tried to envision her future. What would it look like? She would have to figure out a way to make a living. Options for women in this place were very limited. She could be a wife and mother, a whore, or a servant. She had no craft skill that she could capitalize on. She had never been much of a cook so that was off the table. She was a fighter, a warrior, but she did not want to swear fealty to another ruler that would see her indentured for any length of time. A mercenary? Perhaps that would be her only option.

Sophie was speaking to him. With an effort Simon turned toward her and focused on what she was saying.

"You and I are going to have to start on the guest list. We have to consult with Mrs. Abbot to figure out where everyone will stay."

"Sophie," Simon said. He took her hand in his and looked into her eyes. "I want to put these plans on hold."

Sophie sucked in a breath. She pulled her hand out of his.

"I think it would be wise for us not to rush into a marriage. We've known each other for most of our lives, but I am not sure if we are suited to spend the rest of our lives together."

"What are you talking about? I am more than capable to be your queen, Simon."

"I have no doubt that you are, but are you capable of being my woman?" Simon watched her as she processed that question. He was not surprised to see a look of disgust flash across her face.

"I think you are putting too much emphasis on that, Simon. I promised you an heir."

"Yes, you promised me that, but nothing more. I won't live in a loveless marriage."

"That's what dalliances are for. It's too much to expect that we could be satisfied with each other for our entire lives."

"I don't believe that and the fact that you have already thought of it before we are even married is cause for concern to me."

"We can still be happy with each other without sex, Simon. I know I can."

"Well, I can't, Sophie. I am not willing to settle for less. You need to decide what you are willing to give."

Tig's days merged one into the other. She had been on the road for eight weeks. The farther north she went, the fewer people she saw, but she was not alone. Griffin and Juno were her companions, they appreciated her wit and found all her stories fascinating. She couldn't have hoped for better company. Still, she was beginning to miss people.

Her hunting skills had improved. If there was game, she was guaranteed a supper. She had snared a rabbit, cleaned it, and was roasting it on a spit over a small fire when Griffin growled, a low rumble in his chest. Tig sat still, surveying her surroundings. A twig snapped to her right.

"Good evening, friend," a voice said from the bush, the speaker still hidden from sight. "I mean you no harm." He stepped into the light; his empty hands held out. He approached her. Griffin stood, facing him, growling.

"Grif," Tig said. He stopped growling but continued to stand guard.

"That's a big dog you have there. Is he friendly?"

"Not at all. If you mean me no harm, as you say, you will be safe enough." Tig touched Grif; he sat beside her. She nodded to a spot across from her. "Would you like to share my supper?"

"You don't have to ask twice." He smiled as he sat down.

Tig looked him over. He was middle aged and slim.

His clothes were well worn. He carried a pack and had a lute strung across his back, which he took off and laid on his pack. He shoved his hands in front of the fire, rubbing them together. He smiled at her.

"Where are you headed, friend?" he asked.

"Nowhere."

"Then I guess you have a long journey ahead of you. I'm Garon the Fantastic. Perhaps you have heard of me."

Tig smiled. "Sorry, I have not, Garon."

"And you are?"

"No one. I don't have a name."

"No one, going nowhere, with nothing. There may be a tune in there."

"If there is, it's a sad one."

"Your profession, friend?"

"Don't have one yet. My future is unknown."

"I envy you. You are truly free. Your life is an empty page, waiting to be written on by your own hand. That's rather romantic."

Tig laughed. "You and I have very different ideas of romance, Garon."

"Everybody does. That's why life is so fascinating. That rabbit looks pretty cooked to me," he hinted.

"I think so," Tig said. She took the spit off the fire. She pulled one of her sais out and cut the rabbit in half, slicing though the spit at the same time. She held one half out to Garon. He took it eagerly and waved it around, cooling the rabbit.

"That's an odd knife you have there."

"It's a short sword."

"I've never seen one like that before, nor a woman who is so at ease wielding a sword."

Tig bit into her share of the rabbit, choosing not to respond to his last statement.

"Why are you Fantastic Garon? How have you earned your fame?"

"I am a musician, a singer and a storyteller. I have entertained rabble and royalty alike. Like you, I am travelling nowhere, but I am really headed somewhere. Where, though, I don't know. I have heard rumors that there will be a royal wedding in Moregane. Perhaps that is where I will go to see if I can earn some money during the celebration."

Tig stopped eating. She swallowed what she had been chewing. She put her hand on Griffin's head, looking down at him. She was no longer hungry. She wanted to jump on Juno and gallop away from Garon as far and as fast as she could. But she didn't. Simon was no longer any concern of hers. She knew she would hear news of Moregane and Simon in the future. She had better learn to deal with it.

"Really," she croaked out. "Where is Moregane?"

"Many weeks of travel to the south. Who knows, I may miss the festivities but there will be villages along the way. I can always entertain on the street or at an inn. As a matter of fact, as payment for this meal, I will entertain you, friend." He finished his rabbit, licked his fingers, wiped them on his jacket, and picked up his lute. He looked at Tig. "Any requests? What are you in the mood for?"

"Something sweet would be nice," she said.

"I know just the thing," he said. He strummed a few bars, tuned the lute, and started singing.

He had a marvelous, rich voice. Tig lay down, resting her head on Griffin who was splayed on the ground beside her. The music spun a relaxing web around her. She closed her eyes to concentrate on the words and quickly fell asleep.

Tig woke the next morning just as the sun had crested the horizon. It was early. Garon was bundled in a blanket, sleeping with his head on his pack. Quietly, she got up and went for a run. He was still sleeping when she returned to camp. She went into her yoga stretches and then did her sword exercises. She sheathed her sais and turned to find Garon sitting up watching her, a smile on his face.

"I have never seen anything like that before. You are like water, flowing from one movement to the next. I am going to write a song about you, my well-met friend."

Tig laughed. "Go ahead, Garon. How about breakfast? Let's see what we can find. Why don't you get that fire started again?"

Half an hour later Tig returned with a pheasant. The fire was roaring and water was boiling. Garon brewed some tea while she cleaned the bird and trussed it to a spit. While breakfast cooked, Garon told a story about an ogre and a giant, a legend from days gone by, that was funny and sad but with a happy ending to show that love could conquer all.

When breakfast was done, Tig saddled Juno and turned to Garon. He walked to her, took her hand in his and raised it to his lips. "Farewell, friend. Fair weather and easy journey to you."

"Thank you, Garon. It's been a pleasure to spend time with you. Fortune and success to you."

She mounted Juno, gave a salute to Garon, and urged Juno forward, Griffin trotting at their side. It had been nice to have had company. She missed people. She missed Simon most of all.

CHAPTER 11

Simon stood on the rampart watching as Sophie climbed into her carriage. Their relationship was over. Sophie could not give him what he wanted in a lifelong partnership and he was not willing to settle for anything less. He felt a loss in the many years he had spent in the supposition that she would be his wife when he could have been looking for the woman he dreamed about. If such a woman existed, he would find her and marry her.

Sophie's carriage drove through the archway, leaving the castle. He watched until her carriage disappeared into the forest. A solitary rider appeared, a young man. He entered the courtyard and dismounted speaking easily to the groom before entering the castle. Simon left his thoughts behind and went to meet the young man.

Simon entered his office to find the young man in conversation with John. He turned to Simon and smiled. "Sire," the man said as he bowed.

He looked vaguely familiar, but Simon could not place him. He was a good-looking man who was fashionably dressed and at ease in his surroundings.

"Sir," Simon responded.

"I had hoped you would recognize me, Sire. I had heard of your accident. I am your nephew, Gilbert."

Simon's eyes widened in surprise. "Gilbert? No!" He

smiled and opened his arms as he approached him. They embraced briefly. Simon held Gilbert away from him, examining his face. "Yes, I see now. I remember you as quite a bit younger."

"I imagine so. I have returned to assist you, Sire. I have been acting as your assistant and emissary for the past five years."

"Truly?" He looked to John who nodded his head in agreement. "You must be tired from your journey. Why don't you rest and get settled. We will speak after dinner."

Gilbert bowed and left Simon's office. He was glad to be back in Moregane. He had enjoyed his visit home but he was no longer used to being idle, nor having his mother treat him as a boy. He was a man. It had been nice to have her cater to him, for a while, but he had a life in Moregane and he was missing his friends and family here.

Simon and Gilbert met at dinner. They sat at the head table. Gilbert scanned the people, looking toward the door every time someone entered the room.

At last, Simon said, "You are looking for someone, Gilbert, a particular young lady perhaps?" He smiled.

Gilbert looked at Simon. "No, not that." Someone else rushed into the hall late for dinner, a man, who quickly found a chair and began to eat. He turned to Simon. "Where is Lady Tig? I have been looking forward to seeing her."

"Lady Tig?" Simon seemed surprised.

"Yes, Sire. Where is she?"

"She is gone, Gilbert."

"Gone? Did you send her home?"

"No, she left on her own. She stole one of my horses and took my dog with her."

"Juno? Juno has always been her mount, Sire, and Griffin has been her dog since we brought her back from Skree."

"Now that is one of the things I will need your assistance with, nephew. Why would we bring her back from anywhere? From what I have heard of her, it is our good fortune that she decided to leave."

"What do you mean?" Gilbert was shocked at Simon's words.

"She is a dangerous woman. A killer. The people in the palace fear her and yet she walked freely through these halls. There were rumors that she was my woman. But I discounted those. Who is she really, Gilbert, and why did she have so much liberty here?"

Gilbert was dumbfounded. His mouth hung open. The King had no idea who Tig was.

Simon seemed annoyed by Gilbert's amazement. "What?" he demanded.

"Sire, Lady Tig is your heart. You cannot have just let her go. Why did she leave? Where did she go?"

Simon laughed. "My heart! I can assure you, THAT woman—"

Tig's face suddenly flashed through Simon's mind, cutting off his words to Gilbert. He saw her, her eyes filled with passion, looking at him, looking up at him as he plunged into her. He could see her, feel her, she was the woman in his dreams. He looked at Gilbert, realization dawning on him.

"Why did she go?" Gilbert asked. "Wait, I passed a carriage as I was approaching the castle. Was that the Duchess of Crissley? Was she here? Why was she here?"

"I brought her here to plan our wedding. We have been betrothed almost since birth."

"You brought her here? And she came? Gods! No wonder Lady Tig left." Gilbert was shocked.

"I sense that there is a great deal that I do not know, Gilbert. You will fill in the blanks." He pushed his chair back from the table. "Let's go to my office. Now."

Gilbert stood. He followed Simon out of the common room, grabbing a bottle of whiskey on the way out. This was going to be interesting.

Two weeks later Tig came to the end of the road. She was in the small farming village of Walden, in front of The Inn at the End, the only inn, in the only village, she had seen for days. She dismounted and tied Juno to the hitching post. She wore a hooded cloak that covered her from head to toe. It was late in the day and a bit chilly. She was tired, hungry and thirsty. She would get a drink and a bed and then try to figure out what was next for her.

She opened the door and walked into a melee. It seemed everyone was fighting. She closed the door and threw up her arm to block a bottle that had been hurled at someone.

The proprietor stood behind the bar, yelling, "Stop it! You idiots!"

Someone ran up to her, holding a chair, fully prepared to bring it down on her head. Tig crouched down and punched him in the stomach. He doubled over and she hit him again with an uppercut to the jaw, sending him sprawling backward. She spun and kicked another man in the head as he was winding up to punch her. He fell backward, bumping into someone else who turned and lunged at her. Tig formed a fist and jabbed him in the throat. He gagged and fell, trying to catch his breath. Someone else came running at her. She jumped on a table and flew at him. She wrapped her legs around his neck, then swung her body to the side, taking him down with her. He landed heavily, hitting his head on the floor, knocking himself out.

Another man pulled a knife and jabbed at her. She leaned back, avoiding the blade. She kicked and hit his hand. The impact opened his hand and the knife fell to the floor. She crouched down, kicking the knife across the room and swiping her attacker's legs out from under him. He fell awkwardly on his shoulder, grunting when he landed. A chair fell on the table in front of her and broke. She picked up the leg and used it to smash someone over the head; he went down. Tig lunged over his body, poking his opponent in the stomach and then brought the leg up to hit his wrist, making him drop the sword he held.

She spun again, chair leg in hand, to face a man who had been approaching her from behind. He stopped. He looked at the chair leg, then scanned the other men on the floor surrounding her. He held up his hands and backed away from her. She turned in a quick circle. The fighting had stopped. All eyes were on her. She waited for the next attack. No one stepped forward. Eyes were averted. Chairs were picked up and sat on. She dropped the chair leg and walked to the bar.

The proprietor slammed a shot glass in front of her and filled it with whiskey. "On the house, friend. Thank you. How can I repay you?"

Tig pushed the hood off her head, picked up the glass and threw back the whiskey. "You can give me a job."

Shocked silence filled the Inn. A woman had just walked in and taken down seven men without a scratch on her! And now she wanted a job?

The proprietor closed his mouth. He held out his hand. "Collin," he said.

"Tiana," Tig said as she shook his hand. "I'll take a room and meals in exchange for whatever work you have."

"I have to tell you I've never seen anything like you before. You can have a job. I'll give you a room and three meals a day. You'll have to keep these idiots from destroying my place. You can serve meals and drinks. Any income you bring in while in this establishment, well," he raised his eyebrows at Tig as he looked her up and down, "I take 20%."

Tig glared at him, "I won't be earning any income that way. If that's what you're looking for, I'm not the woman for the job."

"No, no," he held up his hands, "it's not a requirement."

"Then we have a deal. I'll start tomorrow. For tonight, I will take a room, a bath, and another whiskey." She put her coins on the bar.

Collin pointed toward the stairs beside the bar. "Take the room at the end of the hall. I'll have a bath brought up." He poured a whiskey for her. "Bruce," he yelled. Bruce came out of the kitchen, wiping his hands on his apron. "A bath for Tiana in the back room. She'll be working here. Tiana, Bruce is our cook and helper. Bruce, Tiana."

Bruce nodded his head at Tiana. He turned back toward the kitchen. "I'll get the water warmed," he said.

Tig picked up the glass of whiskey and carried it to a corner of the Inn. She sipped it slowly, watching as Bruce made numerous trips up and down the stairs with a copper tub and a several pails of water. On his last trip, he nodded at her as he descended the stairs. Tig swallowed the last of her whiskey and climbed the stairs to her hot bath.

It wasn't long before the clean water turned grimy from all the dust that had accumulated on her body and in her hair. She was tired of travelling. It seemed as if she had travelled for a year. She was literally at the end of the road. A decision had to be made—turn left or turn right—a decision she didn't want to make. And, as it turned out, a decision that she didn't have to make. She had a job now and a place to stay. She was going to see how this turned out. She could leave at any time without notice if she didn't like it.

She stood and dried herself off, winding another dry

towel around her head she slid into the soft warm bed and fell into a peaceful sleep.

Simon sat across from Gilbert in his study. He was leaning forward, his elbows on his knees, a glass of whiskey in his hands. He was tired. For hours Gilbert had told him the history of the past six years of his life. He was still trying to process some of it: his brother sentencing him to death; him killing his brother; his relationship with Tig. He knew Gilbert hadn't made it up. He had ready answers to all his questions. Never once did Gilbert hesitate as if grasping for a feasible response to his inquiries. It all seemed so outlandish. What had happened between him and Cameron that had caused the rift between them? That was the one thing that Gilbert could not answer.

But, Tig. That was more fantastic than anything else. Gilbert could not fill in the intimate details of their relationship but there was no question, in his mind, that he had loved her. Simon cringed inwardly at the episode with Sophie. He had betrayed Tig, he must have hurt her to the core when he brought Sophie back to Moregane. It also made him speculate as to Sophie's reasons for coming to Moregane. Did she still love him? Did she covet the Queen's crown? Was she wanting revenge against Tig? The more he thought on that the more ominous Sophie's actions became.

He had accused her of being a whore and then treated her like one when he had summoned her to his chamber. He knew the facts, but he had no emotional response to any of them. He could imagine the hurt that he had caused Tig, he empathized with her, and he hated himself for what he had done to her because he was not that type of a person. He would never intentionally hurt someone he loved. In a way he was relieved that she was gone so that he would not have to face her in the morning knowing what he now knew.

He drained his glass, leaned back in his chair, and blew out a breath.

"What are we going to do about Lady Tig?" Gilbert asked.

Simon looked at him. "Nothing, Gilbert. There is nothing to do. I don't know where she is. I feel nothing for her. Why would I want to bring her back here? I have nothing to offer her."

"But, Sire..."

"No. I feel nothing for her. I cannot in good conscious bring her back here for nothing. She would expect me to be something that I am not. To give her something that I cannot offer. It's best this way. Don't you think so?"

"When you put it forth in those terms, I have to agree," he said sadly. "I will miss her, Sire. I miss her now."

"That's the problem, Gilbert. I don't."

CHAPTER 12

Word of Tiana spread like fire through the village. A woman who had broken up a fight at the Inn, and she worked there now. Collin's business picked up in the next few weeks as villagers came to see Tiana. Some of them tested her but she was quick and dangerous. There were no more fights in the Inn. Arguments were quickly quelled and, if they progressed, fights were taken outside.

Tiana, herself, was a bright spot in the old Inn. She was attractive and witty. She enjoyed working with the public and became an additional draw to the Inn, having smiles for the regulars and kind words for others. There was no additional income to be earned from her though. She definitely did not share her charms with anyone.

Tobias heard about Tiana but had not been to the Inn for a while. He met some friends at the Inn one night. Tiana came to their table to take their order. She was indeed beautiful. Tobias smiled at her and she returned the smile. She returned with a pitcher of ale, pouring their mugs. She took their money, smiled again, and turned to leave. Tobias, grabbed her arm, spun her onto his lap and shoved his hand down her bodice, gripping her breast.

He laughed. "I've got something special for you, darling. What say we go to your room?" Words he had spoken in the past that always ended in a room with his cock in some comely wench.

Suddenly, he stiffened and leaned back in his chair. Tiana had a knife at his throat. "You should rethink the placement of your hand, sweetness," she said.

Tobias was frozen. The Inn came to a standstill, all eyes on their table.

Tiana leaned into him and whispered in his ear. His face drained of color. He jerked his hand out of her dress. Tiana calmly stood, sheathed her knife, smoothed her dress and walked away.

His friends leaned forward. "What did she say to you?" they demanded.

"She said…" He shook his head to clear his thoughts. "She said that she had killed more men than I had met in my entire life. Then she asked if I wanted to be the next one."

His friends all looked at Tiana with amazement in their eyes. Some of them started to smirk and were about to say something when Tobias added, "I believed her."

That was the next story about Tiana that circulated in the village.

Simon stretched lazily under the covers. Another day. He sat up, swinging his feet off the bed and onto the floor. Mentally, he went through the list of things that needed to be done. He was in a good mood. He stood and walked to the wardrobe and pulled out a shirt.

Maybe he wouldn't work all day long. He would take a

long lunch. He would find Tig, interrupt her training, maybe order a picnic lunch, go for a ride, and make love to her in the forest. He felt as if he hadn't seen her in a long time. He smiled as he thought of her. That's what he needed, some Tig time. He felt confident she would welcome the interruption and his attention. As a matter of fact, he owed her a fuck from the battle yester—

The room spun around him. He put his hand out, grabbing a chair. He sat as everything came rushing back to him—the past six years of his life that had gone missing were suddenly there. Everything that Gilbert had told him was true, it was exactly as Gilbert had said. He gripped the arms of the chair. What had he done? He groaned. He knew what he had done. He had caused Tig to run away with his callous treatment of her and then he had brought Sophie to Moregane to plan their wedding! He smacked the side of his hand with his fist as the depth of his stupidity hit him. By the gods, he was an ass!

Following on the heels of this revelation was the absolute sense of loss that he felt. Tig would never forgive him for this, would she? He had betrayed her. He had treated her like she was nothing and called her a whore.

Oh, she would be angry. She might even kill him for it. He smiled when he thought of her angry. That was when he loved her most. Truth be told, he was looking forward to their reunion because he would find her, he would apologize to her, and he would make her love him again.

He finished dressing and left his room in a hurry. He strode through the halls and down the stairs. He pushed open the door to Memron's lair, slamming it against the wall.

Simon winced at the smell of this lair. It was dimly lit with a cell in the corner, unoccupied at this moment. He didn't know why Memron needed a cell and he didn't want to know. There were shelves crammed with jars. Some of the things in the jars were moving. There were small cages hung from the rafters with small creatures. Simon felt uncomfortable in this room. He thought this was maybe only the second time he had ever been here.

Memron jumped at the crash. He turned to see the King bearing down on him. He paled.

"Memron," Simon said, stopping in front of him.

"Sire," Memron squeaked. "Can I help you?"

"Memron," Simon repeated, "you must find Lady Tig."

"I didn't realize she was missing."

"Well, she is, and you are going to find her. I don't care if you have to go and look for her yourself, but you will find her. I want her found now. Do whatever it is that you do and find her."

Memron bowed. "Yes, Sire."

Simon left, slamming the door behind him.

Memron set to work immediately. He stood behind his cauldron and began to throw in herbs, insect carcasses, and various elements. All the ingredients were assembled.

He closed his eyes and began to chant, arcane words rising and falling. A gentle whisper began to rise from the cauldron. Memron spoke louder. The whisper rose in volume.

A dragonfly rose from the cauldron and landed on the rim, slowly beating its wings. It was joined by another and then another and another. The sound of beating wings rose, drowning out Memron's words. The first dragonfly rose into the air and flew out the window, followed by a river of dragonflies streaming through the window and into the sky.

At last, Memron stopped chanting. He sagged. All he had to do was wait. He hoped it would not be long before he received word of Tig's whereabouts.

Tig needed a man. Tension was building in her and no matter how hard or often she worked out she couldn't rid herself of the need. It was not that she lacked offers. Old Ned proposed to her almost daily. Other proposals had come her way from young men wanting to settle down and start families. She was not ready for that kind of commitment. She was not sure she ever would be.

She sat in the sunshine in front of the Inn, Griffin at her feet. "If only I could kiss you and make you my prince," she teased. He looked at her, perking up his ears. Griffin as a man would be tall and muscular, kind and gentle. She ruffled the wiry hair on his head and sighed. A shadow fell across Griffin, she looked up and gasped. There he was!

Mathan was tall and well-muscled. He didn't come to the village often and it was a treat for him to stop at the Inn for a meal and an ale. He saw the woman sitting outside with her dog. He thought she was the most beautiful woman he had ever seen. He nodded to her and entered the Inn.

"Tiana," Collin yelled from inside.

"Coming," she replied.

She stood and entered the Inn. Collin nodded his head toward where Mathan sat, his legs barely fitting under the table. She smiled and went to his table.

"Good afternoon," she said and smiled.

Mathan gaped at her. She was smiling at him. He quickly returned the smile. "Good afternoon," he replied.

"What can I get for you?"

"What are you serving today?"

"Rabbit stew or leg of lamb."

"I'll take the stew and an ale please."

"All right then. I'll be right back."

Tig went to the kitchen and waited while the cook filled a bowl with stew. She put the bowl on a plate and added several thick slices of bread. When she left the kitchen, Collin had already pulled the ale and placed the mug on the corner of the bar. She picked it up and carried the meal to Mathan, placing it in front of him. He paid her and she went to the bar and gave the money to Collin. She picked up a cloth, went to the table beside Mathan and began to wipe down the table and chairs.

"I haven't seen you here before," she said.

"I don't come to the village often," he said.

"Do you live far away?"

"Not far, a half hour on horseback."

"I'm Tiana."

"Mathan."

"How's the stew, Mathan?"

"Good. It always is. Did you make it?"

"Me?" Tig laughed. "If you can eat it, I didn't make it."

Mathan laughed along with her, meeting her eyes. Tig saw the interest there.

Tig pulled out a chair and leaned down to wipe it off, making sure that Mathan was watching and letting him look down her dress. She looked up at him and smiled again.

"See something interesting?" she asked.

Mathan's face turned bright red. He looked away.

Tig pushed the chair under the table. Mathan wiped his bowl with the last piece of bread and stuffed it into his mouth.

"Are you married, Mathan?"

"No."

"I find that hard to believe, a man like you still single."

Mathan didn't know what to do or what to say. Tiana was a beautiful woman and she seemed to be flirting with him. Was it because there was no one else in the Inn at this time? Maybe so.

The door opened and Old Ned came in, sitting in his usual chair.

"I'll be right back. I promise," Tig said as she went to the bar. Collin poured a whiskey. Tig took it to Ned. He paid her. She took the money to Collin and went back to Mathan's table.

"Are you still hungry? Do you want anything else?" She winked at him.

"I'll have another ale," he said.

Tig picked up his plate and mug. She placed the mug on the bar. "Another one," she said to Collin as she walked into the kitchen dropping off the plates. She came back out, picked up the mug, and took it to Mathan's table.

"Do you want some company? Do you mind if I sit with you?"

"Not at all, please do."

Collin shot a quizzical look at her. She sat down beside Mathan.

"What do you do, Mathan?"

"I'm a farmer."

"Really?" she gushed. She placed her hand on his arm. "What kind of farming do you do?"

"A little bit of everything. I've got some crops, a few pigs, sheep, chickens."

"That's so exciting! Do you love it?" Tig couldn't believe the words that were coming out of her mouth, but she couldn't stop herself. She was going to have Mathan. If not tonight, then very soon.

"I like it, aye. I do well enough to support myself with some extra to sell or trade."

Tig leaned against Mathan, pressing her breasts into his arm. "I'm so glad you came in today. It's so nice to have met you."

Mathan blushed again. "You as well, Tiana."

The door opened again, more customers coming in for a meal and some liquor. She pouted. "I've got to get to work,

Mathan. I hope I get to see you again." She stood and hurried away before he could respond.

CHAPTER 13

Mathan was back the next day. It was early in the day and Tig was sitting outside again with Grif. She was leaning against the wall of the Inn, her eyes closed. Suddenly the sun disappeared. She opened her eyes. Mathan stood in front of her. She smiled up at him. He held out his hand. He had a small bouquet of flowers. She took them from him and held them up to her face.

"They are beautiful, Mathan, thank you."

"Not as beautiful as you, Tiana."

"Really, do you mean that?"

"Every word."

She smiled. She reached out her hand. He took her hand in his and she pulled herself up. Holding his hand, she led him behind the Inn to the stable. She led him inside where it was dark and cool.

He put his hands on her hips. She stood on her toes and kissed him lightly on the lips. Mathan took her into his arms and kissed her passionately. Tig pressed herself against him, hoping this would get better.

Mathan's lips were soft. There was no urgency in his kiss. There was no electricity between them, like there was with…. No, she would not even think his name. He was in her past and out of her reach now.

Tig put her hand on Mathan's crotch. She felt his cock

respond. She rubbed his erection. Mathan groaned, continuing to kiss her. She gently pushed him off her and undid his pants. His cock sprung out at her. She looked at it. It would do. She lay down on the hay bales and lifted her skirts, spreading her legs. Mathan fell on her and slid into her. He pushed into her and was finished in no time.

Inwardly, Tig sighed. "You were wonderful, Mathan," she said as she stood, pushing her skirts down. "Why don't you come back when I'm finished work? We can do this again. Would you like that?"

Mathan smiled. "Yes."

"Tiana," Collin yelled from inside the Inn.

"Gotta go," she said. She leaned down and kissed him on the lips.

Mathan watched her walk away, surely feeling like the luckiest man in the world.

"It's been a week, Memron," Simon said. "Any news?"

"No, Sire, not yet."

"It's been a week," Simon repeated.

"It could be that Lady Tig has travelled farther afield than we expected," he reasoned.

"Yes, that could be the case."

Simon was disappointed that there was no word of Tig's location. He was also hurt at the possibility that she had run as far away from him as she could possibly go. He missed her. He yearned for her. He would leave right now if he could, but where would he go? Should he go north or south? East or west? If he picked a direction, should he go straight or turn at any point? Would she stay where she stopped or would she continue to move? He could spend the rest of his life looking for her and he would if he had to.

Mathan entered the Inn just as Tig was finishing her shift. She smiled when she saw him enter. This had been so easy, she thought. She wiped down the last table, pushing the chairs in. She caught Mathan's eye and cocked her head, signaling for him to meet her outside. He nodded and left. She followed him outside. She took his hand in hers and looked up at him.

"Do you want to take me to your home?" she asked.

He didn't hesitate. "Yes."

"Just let me saddle my horse," she said.

He unhitched his mount and followed her back to the stables. He waited silently as she quickly saddled Juno and led her out of the stable. She mounted and followed Mathan out of the village, Griffin trotting behind them.

The ride was short and quiet. Mathan was not a talkative man. They took their horses to a fenced-in lean-to and quickly unsaddled and groomed them before releasing them.

"Come," Mathan said as he turned and walked toward his cottage, Tig following behind him. He opened the door and let Tig proceed him into the one room cottage. His cottage was small but well kept. It was sparsely furnished but neat and organized.

"This is lovely," Tig said.

Mathan smiled at her.

Tig walked up to him and began to unbutton his shirt. He pulled his shirt over his head. Next, she undid his pants and slid them down his hips. He stood naked before her. He was a marvelous specimen. She put her hand on his chest and ran it down to his belly. He was already erect.

She stepped away from him, undid the laces on her dress and let it slide down to pool on the floor. Next, she undid the tie on her shift and let it fall onto the floor.

Mathan reached out one hand, cupping and squeezing her breast, his breath ragged. With his other hand, he hooked her waist and pulled her toward him. He leaned down and kissed her hungrily. Tig pulled away, took his hand and led him to the bed in the corner of the room. She pushed him down on the bed. She took his hard cock in her hand and guided it into herself as she straddled him. She took his hands and placed them on her breasts as she began to rock. He squeezed her breasts and pushed into her.

This was nice, Tig thought. Mathan dropped his hands and grabbed her ass. He began to pump into her vigorously. He was going to come. No, Tig thought, not yet. But it was too late. He came. Tig rolled off him and lay down beside him. He lay on his side, looking at her.

"I love you, Tiana," he said before he flopped onto his back and fell asleep.

Oh no, Tig thought. She pulled a blanket over them and rolled onto her side, away from Mathan. He's going to take some work, she thought, before she drifted off to sleep.

She woke late in the morning. Mathan was not there. She sat up, pulling the blanket around her shoulders. She stood. There was a plate on the table with some bread and cheese. He had left it out for her. She went to the stove where a small fire was still burning. She put the kettle on and waited for the water to boil. She made a cup of tea and sat at the table nibbling at the bread and cheese.

Mathan opened the door and walked in. "Good morning, Tiana," he said.

She smiled at him. "Is it still morning?"

He thought she looked beautiful. Her hair was a mess, she hadn't been awake long he thought. She had the blanket wrapped around her, her bare shoulders evidence that she was naked underneath.

"Barely," he said. "I thought I would let you sleep late."

"I appreciate that, Mathan."

"I fed your horse and your dog. Been busy with the other livestock."

"Thank you for that and the breakfast. That was thoughtful of you. Why don't you join me for some tea?" she invited.

He nodded, poured himself a cup and sat across from her.

Tig stood and walked toward him. She undid his pants and took his cock in her hand. He was hard instantly. She dropped the blanket and sat on him. She took his head in her hands. She began to rock. "Tell me, in as much detail as you can, about your sheep. Don't stop talking until I tell you."

"Well, I don't know what you want me to tell you," he

said. He didn't want to talk at this moment. He would rather concentrate on fucking her.

"Tell me how you care for them from the moment they are born," Tig said.

He began speaking, telling her about lambing season. His voice was deep and soothing. She put her hands on his shoulders, continuing to rock. Mathan put his hands on her ass. He stopped speaking.

"Don't stop talking," Tig demanded. "Tell me more."

He told her that lambs weaned from their mothers after about two months. That they were very playful.

Tig began to bounce on his lap. She was getting close.

"Keep talking," she ground out through clenched teeth.

He started to speak about shearing season and selling the wool. He faltered and grabbed her breast. Tig moaned. She rocked forward, rubbing her clit on his cock. Mathan started to push into her. No more words were spoken as they both worked their way toward climax. He thrust into her two more times. They came together. Tig wrapped her arms around his neck, riding the waves crashing through her body as Mathan stroked her back.

A short time later she stood and began to get dressed.

"I've got to get back to the village," she said as she did up the laces on her dress.

"Are you coming back," Mathan asked.

"Do you want me to?"

"Yes."

"Then I guess I am."

He smiled, nodded, and left. When Tig was dressed she went to the paddock. Mathan had saddled Juno. He stood, waiting for her, reins in hand. She lifted her face to his. He looked at her, then comprehension set in. He bent down and kissed her. She mounted Juno and rode to the village.

CHAPTER 14

Simon barged into Memron's lair, the door banging against the wall.

Memron jumped. "Quickly, close the door, Sire," he said.

Simon turned, grabbed the handle and slammed the door shut.

"They're returning. We will learn something," Memron said. "Come, look."

Memron was standing in front of his cauldron, leaning over and looking into it. Simon came to stand beside him, looking into the cauldron as well. Whatever was in there was silver and smooth as glass. A dragonfly hovered over the cauldron and then dove into it. The mixture rippled slightly, closing over the dragonfly. A picture began to emerge. A road, bordered by trees. The picture moved, following the road. A group of travelers appeared. The image zoomed in closer to the travelers. It was a group of men. They rode silently.

Another dragonfly appeared, hovering momentarily before diving into the mixture. The picture changed. They were in a market. There were stalls of produce, cages with chickens and rabbits, stalls with goods. People were milling about, buying and selling goods.

Yet another dragonfly appeared and dove into the

mixture. The picture showed a road leading to a village. They passed through the village, approaching a church on the outskirts, singing in the air.

Another dragonfly. Mountains, a river, someone fishing. Another dragonfly. Forest, a herd of deer, a clearing, rays of sunshine lighting it.

Simon watched for what seemed like hours, his eyes getting bleary from watching the pictures change. He recognized some places but most of the pictures showed wilderness and wild animals. He closed his eyes. He couldn't stand here forever. There were other things that had to be done. It could be days before any sign of Tig appeared.

Just one more, he thought to himself. It was getting dark; the sun was setting. A small family sat around a fire cooking.

"Hello, friends," someone said.

The husband stood, pulling his sword. The children ran to stand behind their mother.

"I mean no harm," a man said as he emerged from the brush. "I am Garon the Fantastic. I will entertain you in exchange for a meal and some company," he offered.

The husband and wife exchanged a look. "You may join us, Garon. We could use some entertainment, but all we have to offer is a humble meal."

"My favorite," Garon said as he found a spot and sat.

Simon watched as they ate their meal exchanging pleasantries. Garon did some simple tricks for the children, then sang a song.

"I met a beautiful woman in my travels," he said. "She

is a lady of mystery. A woman with no name going nowhere," his voice lowered, "but deadly."

Simon leaned closer to the cauldron.

"She was accompanied by a huge gray beast, eyes as yellow as amber, teeth as large as my finger. A hound from hell I would wager. He would have torn my throat out save for a magic command from its mistress!"

Simon gasped. That beast must be Griffin. If that was Griffin, then the mystery woman had to be Tig! For the first time in weeks, he felt hope flutter in his chest.

The children shrieked. "Oh, do not worry, when we parted, she was headed in the opposite direction, and it must have been a good two months ago. Whoever she was she is long gone."

A dragonfly dove into the cauldron. The picture changed, another village. Simon swore.

"Bring him back," he ordered Memron.

"I cannot, Sire. It's too late."

Simon raked his hair back from his forehead. "He said that was two months ago that he saw them. How long ago did that dragonfly witness this meeting?"

"I would guess it was 10 days ago, Sire."

Simon tried to do some calculations. Garon met Tig at least two months ago. He told that story ten days ago. Simon came to no conclusion. Where had Garon been when he met Tig. Where was he now?

Tig rode to Mathan's home at a slow pace. She held the last of the day's stew in a jar, something for Mathan for supper.

She smiled as she thought back on her day at the Inn. Rumor had spread that she had spent the night at Mathan's house. More than one patron had mentioned Mathan's name to her that day in the hope that she would provide more information. She would simply smile and quickly change the subject.

The day was coming to an end, the shadows lengthening. She could see the gate to Mathan's farm ahead of her. Mathan stood at the gate, looking down the road. When he saw her, he waved and started to walk toward her. Tig spurred Juno into a trot. When she reached Mathan, he took Juno's reins, bringing her to a stop. He walked to Tig and lifted her down.

"I'm happy to see you, Tiana." He smiled as he greeted her.

"You are so thoughtful, Mathan," she responded. "I have the last of the day's stew for your supper."

Together they walked into the yard and to the paddock where Mathan stripped Juno of her saddle and bridle. He rubbed her down, released her and dumped a small pail of oats for her dinner. He then turned to Tig and walked with her to the cottage.

Tig warmed up the last of the stew and cut up some bread. She served Mathan his dinner and sat with him. Together they talked about the day, Mathan describing his duties around the farm and Tig informing him of the gossip in the village concerning them.

"I hope you do not suffer from these rumors, Tiana," he said, looking at her.

"How can I suffer? People talk, there is nothing I can do about it."

"But your reputation…."

"Fuck my reputation. I have dealt with far worse than this type of gossip," she said cryptically.

"What do you mean?"

"Nothing for you to worry about, Mathan, all of that is in my past. What I want to know about is your crops. Tell me about farming Mathan, how do you start a crop?" Tig began to undress, Mathan's eyes following her every movement. "How do you care for your crops?" Tig removed her dress. "When do you harvest them?" She untied her shift and let it fall to the floor. "Do you sell your crops?"

She approached Mathan and held out her hand. He took her hand and stood. Tig led him to the bed and began to undress him. "Tell me, Mathan, tell me everything."

Mathan began to speak. "I begin working the soil as early as possible in the spring." He lifted his shirt over his head. "As soon as the soil is dry enough, I hook the ox to the plow and till the soil." Tig unbuttoned his pants and slid them down his hips. He was already erect. She pushed him back onto the bed. "I plant the seeds." He reached up for her breasts. Tig straddled him, guiding his cock into her.

"Don't stop talking, Mathan, tell me more," she instructed as she began to gyrate her hips.

Mathan grabbed her and rolled her over until she was underneath him. "I hope for favorable weather—rain, but not too much." He pushed into her. "Warm days and sun." He pushed into her again. Tig wrapped her legs around his waist. "It takes three months for a good…" he pushed into her, "…crop." He stopped talking and began to fuck her, his tempo increasing. Tig met his every thrust, pleasure building in her body.

"When do you harvest," Tig panted.

"In the fall. Tiana," he grunted.

"And then?"

"Enough talking," he growled. He bent down and kissed her. He closed his eyes, arched his back and began to pound into her with powerful strokes that jolted her body.

Tig began to moan. This was nice. If Mathan could maintain his composure for another couple of minutes, it would be a happy ending for both of them. She could feel her climax approaching. Her body began to tense. Mathan pumped into her one last time with a mighty shout before collapsing beside her. He was asleep within minutes.

Tig lay beside him. She had been so close. She slid her hands down, over her belly, and found her nub. She began to rub her clit. She closed her eyes, feeling the sensation build. Her body tensed, she was going to come. She rubbed her clit furiously, gritting her teeth, holding her breath. Suddenly, she saw Simon's face, smiling at her. For a moment she held that image, arched her back and came. She lay still as waves of pleasure washed over her.

Mathan rolled over in his sleep, his arm draping across her. Tig's eyes flew open. Simon disappeared. She rolled onto her side, pushing her ass into Mathan's stomach. His grip tightened around her. The warmth of Mathan's body and the dying fire in the stove lulled her into a sound sleep.

CHAPTER 15

A week later, Memron scurried into Simon's office.

"Sire, I have news," he said, excitement in his voice.

Simon looked up from the ledger he was reviewing, expectation written on his face. "Tell me," he ordered.

"I have seen her and the dog. She looks well."

"Where did you see her?"

"She is at The End, Sire."

"The End? What is that? Where is that?"

"I do not know. I merely saw a sign that said 'The End'."

Simon looked at John. "Does that sound familiar to you? Have you heard of such a place."

"No, Sire, to both questions," John replied.

"There is something else, Your Majesty," Memron said.

Simon looked at him. Memron was wringing his hands. He looked uncomfortable.

"What else, Memron?"

"There is a man, Sire, Lady Tig was with a man."

"What do you mean she was with a man? Does she appear to be in danger?" Once out of his mouth, those words sounded ludicrous. Tig would not be in danger from a man, any man. He glanced at Memron who was nervously watching him. Why would Memron be nervous about Tig being with a man, unless… "She's with a man," he repeated, realization dawning him.

"Yes, Sire."

Tig was with a man. She had found a man. Had she replaced him? Simon rejected the thought as soon as it popped into his head. She could not replace him! She could not have found another man that connected with her in the same manner as he did. Impossible! He would find her and she would realize that they were meant for each other. He swore it.

On second thought…she had replaced him so quickly? Did their relationship mean nothing to her to have shed herself of him so fast? He was…angry. Who was this man? Was he a king? Simon doubted that. He didn't doubt that Tig was sharing her body with this man. Could he pleasure her as he could? Impossible. Did he know Tig's body as only he did? Never.

Why would she have cast him aside so quickly? Because he was supposed to be married to Sophie by now. He certainly didn't expect her to swear to a life of celibacy without him could he? Why not? Don't be ridiculous he chided himself.

The more he thought of Tig and another man the angrier he got. He turned to Memron, rage written on his face. "Find her now," he bellowed.

Memron bowed to his King and, walking backward, he scurried out of Simon's office and back to his lair.

Mathan and Tig easily fell into a routine. Mathan would

rise before the sun, have a quick breakfast, and leave to tend to his animals and the farm. As soon as he left, Tig would get up. She would go for a run and then into a copse of trees on Mathan's property where she would practice with her sais, returning to the cottage before lunch. Mathan would meet her for lunch, then saddle Juno and bring her to the cottage for Tig to leave for her job at the Inn. When Tig returned in the evening, Mathan would walk out to meet her, and together they would walk to the paddock to unsaddle Juno and have supper, usually food that Tig brought back from the Inn.

Eventually, Tig learned all there was to know about running Mathan's farm in an attempt to increase his stamina in bed. Mathan was improving but more often than not Tig would have to find her own release after he fell asleep.

Tig was not dissatisfied with the life she was leading. She had even developed feelings of affection for Mathan. He was kind and gentle. He was considerate of her, always saddling Juno for her, always waiting for her return from the Inn. She knew he loved her but her feelings for him were not love.

She worked hard at not thinking about Simon or Moregane because, if she did, a restlessness would come over her, the desire to fight would begin to burn in her blood, and there was nowhere here for her to find that release. When those thoughts did creep into her mind and she found, for whatever reason, that she was powerless to stop them, she would have to tamp them down until the next morning when she would punish herself with an extra-long run. She would imagine Sophie's face while she practiced with her throwing stars, landing each one into the imagined space between Sophie's eyes.

Time was passing and Simon was no closer to finding Tig. He had asked Gilbert if he had ever heard of The End, which he had not. He had tasked the guards to ask any travelers coming into Moregane if they knew of The End, no one had. He scoured every map in his library for mention of The End. He had John send out letters to Moregane's allies inquiring if they had any knowledge of a place known as The End. He had not received any responses, granted most of those letters had not reached their destinations yet. Each day that passed, Simon worried that Tig would be replacing him with the man that she had found.

Simon had finished his work for the day. He was on his way to his chamber to clean up and change before dinner. He was passing through the common room when one of the guards approached him.

"Sire," the guard bowed, "a man has come seeking a few nights of employment. He is an entertainer. He calls himself Garon the Fantastic."

Simon knew that name. He had to think for a moment why it was familiar to him and when he realized that that was the man he had seen in Memron's cauldron, he ordered the guard to bring Garon to his office at once. Gilbert was nearby. He motioned for Gilbert to join him in his office.

• • •

Garon was ushered into Simon's office by two guards. He was placed in front of a young man sitting in a chair. The room was mostly in shadow, the fireplace the only light illuminating a small circle that included the young man.

The guards turned and left, closing the doors behind them. Truth be told, Garon was nervous. He had never been escorted by guards before. He wondered if he was in some sort of trouble. Perhaps he had broken a law that he was unaware of. He had been in that predicament before and it had taken some fast talking on his part to avoid punishment.

"Sir," Garon said, bowing before the man who'd been introduced as Gilbert.

"You are Garon the Fantastic?" Gilbert asked.

"Indeed I am. I am seeking a few nights employment, I am a magician, a singer, a musician…"

"And a storyteller," a voice said from the darkness.

Garon spun around. There was a tall man standing in the shadows. Garon had not noticed him when he was ushered in.

"Yes, sir, a storyteller as well."

"Then, Garon, tell us a story," the man in the chair said.

Garon turned to look at him. "I would be pleased to, sirs." He cast a glance at the man behind him, trying to address both men. "Do you have a request?"

Gilbert leaned forward, resting his elbows on his knees. He looked at Simon, then back at Garon. "Tell us about the woman you met in the woods."

"I have met many women in the woods, sirs. Do you mean Lillith the enchantress, although I must confess it is not truly my story, I have borrowed it from another—"

"The woman with the large gray dog," the voice in the darkness said.

"I don't recall a woman with a large gray dog," Garon responded.

"The woman with no name, going nowhere, with a large beast with teeth as long as your fingers," Simon said.

"A woman with no name... a large gray dog..."

Suddenly the man rushed out of the darkness and grabbed Garon's shirt. "Think man. Tell us that story."

Garon was speechless. He looked into the man's eyes, at the impatience there. He tried to think about the story he was requesting—a woman with no name, going nowhere.

Suddenly, it dawned on him. The man must have realized, because he released Garon, poured a small glass of whiskey, handed it to him, and said, "Tell me."

Garon gulped down the whiskey. "There is not much to tell, sirs. I met her one evening many months ago. She was camped in the woods with a huge gray dog and her horse. She said she had no name and that she was going nowhere. I offered to entertain her in exchange for a meal."

"Why then would she have stayed in your memory? As you have said, you have met many women in the woods."

"For one thing, sirs, she was one of the most beautiful women I have ever seen. But the next morning, while she thought I was still asleep, she was practicing her swordplay. It was a sight to behold. I have never seen anything like it before. She moved as one with her swords, almost too fast to see, and silent. I told her I would write a song about her and... yes, that's right, she said it would be a sad story to tell."

Gilbert looked at the man. "She can only be Tig, Sire."

The man nodded his agreement. He looked at Garon again. "Where did you meet her?"

"I cannot say. It was months and months ago. In the forest. There were no markers. I can hardly recall myself where I was. All I can say is it was in the north."

"Did she say where she was going," the man asked.

"Nowhere. That's what she said, she was going nowhere."

"In what direction did she go when she left you?"

"I believe she was continuing to travel north."

Gilbert asked the next question. "Where would she have ended up if she continued travelling north do you suppose?"

"Let's see, the farther north you go the villages are fewer and farther between, small hamlets really: Crested, Nob's Hill, St. Michael's Post. If she didn't stop anywhere, why she would come to The End."

"What did you say?" the man barked.

"The End. She would come to The End."

"Where is that?" the man demanded.

"North, Sir. Take the road north until it runs out. It will stop at the Inn at The End, or simply The End in the town of Walden."

The man looked at Gilbert, who said, "I will make arrangements, Sire. We will leave at first light."

The man spoke to Garon. "I thank you for your assistance Garon. You will be free to stay here until you are ready to leave. Payment of my gratitude to you."

Garon bowed to the man. "Thank you, sir, for your hospitality."

CHAPTER 16

Tig was in the copse of trees on Mathan's property. She had just ended a long, hard run. She had her sword in hand and, discarding all form, was hacking away at a tree. She was being forced to make a decision and she was annoyed.

Last night, as usual, Mathan had met her on the road at the gate to his farm. He had walked with her to the paddock to tend to Juno before feeding her and releasing her. Together they went into the cottage for dinner. Mathan was sopping up the last of the stew in his bowl with a piece of bread when he broached the topic, again.

"Tiana, I love you. I have told you countless times. It is time for us to get married."

"We don't need to get married, Mathan. Things are fine the way they are, aren't they?"

"Yes, they are fine the way they are, but what about our children? No child of mine will be born a bastard."

"What child? Are you pregnant, Mathan?"

"Don't be ridiculous, Tiana, it was funny the first time you said that. Don't change the topic. I want children. I want you to be the mother of my children. I want us to start a family."

"I don't want a family. We can be happy together, just the two of us."

"It's the natural order of things, Tiana. We fall in love,

we get married, and we have children. That is how the world works."

"Not my world, Mathan. I am not ready to have children."

"Don't you love me?"

How could she answer that? She didn't love him. She had looked into his eyes, not knowing what to say and he had read the truth. There was a heartbreaking moment of awkward silence. He pushed his chair away from the table and went outside.

Tig followed him out. She stood next to him at the paddock. Juno trotted over to her. Tig stroked her soft nose.

"You don't know me, Mathan. If you did, you might feel very differently about me."

"I know you, Tiana. I love you."

"You only know the me that I let you see. There are things in my past..."

"That doesn't matter to me," he said as he took her in his arms. "The past is over. You are with me now. I love the Tiana that I know."

"That's the thing, Mathan, you don't know my past and because of that you don't know me."

He held her away from him, "I will say it again, Tiana, I love you. I want us to have children. If you deny me that I can't see a future for us."

Tig sheathed her sword and pulled out her sais. She continued her relentless attack on the poor tree in front of her. She was angry. If she wanted to stay with Mathan, she was going to have to marry him and bear his children.

What if she denied him? She could always return to the Inn, her room would still be available to her, but she would lose the intimate relationship she had with Mathan, mediocre as it was. She could find another man, easily, if she wanted to, but did she want to?

She could also leave Mathan and the village. Maybe she had stayed on long enough. Maybe she should move on. Maybe she could become a mercenary. That had always been an option for her.

Suddenly a twig snapped behind her. In an instant, she dropped one of her sais, pulled out a star, and threw it in the direction of the noise. She followed the star with her eyes and saw it stick into a sapling, mere inches away from Mathan's head.

Mathan turned to look at the star embedded in the sapling. His eyes wide, he turned and looked at her.

Calmly she returned his gaze and said, in a steady voice, "Don't ever sneak up on me again."

Simon and Gilbert had been on the road for months. They travelled at a steady pace, making as many miles in a day as they possibly could. Simon had to hand it to Tig, though; when she ran away, she ran away, far away. As the weeks passed, the towns grew smaller and farther apart, as did the travelers they met on the road.

They did stop for meals in the villages they passed. The closer they got to the end of the road, they were able to confirm that, yes, the Inn at The End did exist but, no, no one had heard of Tig. Simon began to fear that perhaps she hadn't stayed there. Perhaps she had stopped for a while and then travelled on. Where would she go to next? Would he ever find her if she had moved on? He shared his fears with Gilbert, but Gilbert did not have any reassuring words for him.

Tig was back in her room at the Inn. After the incident in the woods, Mathan had begun to look at her strangely and behave cautiously around her. That was when Tig knew their relationship was over.

Everyone in the village knew the same day that she moved back to the Inn. Her regular patrons offered condolences on her breakup. Old Ned, though, offered no condolences and, again, proposed to her before he left when the Inn closed. Again, she refused.

She missed Mathan. She missed his company and his kindness to her, but she didn't yearn for him. It never crossed her mind to return to him and beg his forgiveness or agree to his terms. What she missed most of all though, was his cock and her regular use of it.

Gilbert and Simon opened the door to the Inn and entered, glad to have finally reached their destination. Dusty and travel worn, Simon removed his hat and headed to the bar, Gilbert behind him. It was Friday night and it was busy. It was the Fall Festival and the village and bar were bustling with people. All the tables in the Inn were taken, it was standing room only. A fiddler played in the corner of the room. The drinks were flowing and people were happy, laughing and yelling at each other over the noise.

They approached the bar and ordered two glasses of whiskey. Collin set the glasses on the bar and poured the drinks.

"I'm here to see Tig," Simon said.

"Never heard of 'im," Collin replied.

"Maybe because she isn't a him."

"Never heard of her either," Collin replied.

Off to the side a woman backed out of the kitchen carrying a tray laden with dishes. She stopped momentarily at the bar and picked up two tankards of beer that were sitting on the edge of the bar before heading toward the back of the Inn.

"Tiana," Collin yelled, "you know anyone by the name of Tig?" He turned to Simon and Gilbert. "If anyone would know her, Tiana would."

Tig momentarily faltered on her way to deliver the meals when Collin yelled out to her.

Simon knew immediately that Tiana was Tig. He kept his eyes on her and asked Collin, "Is she armed? Does she carry any weapons?"

Collin chuckled. "Armed? No. She is her own weapon."

Tig delivered the meals to the appropriate tables. She set the tray down and, still holding the tankards of ale, she turned toward the bar. Her eyes met Simon's. He looked at her, one eyebrow raised, watching as anger transformed her.

She glared at him with eyes as dark as flint, her body tensed, her lips thinned. Gods, she was beautiful.

Those who had been watching her and witnessed the transformation fell silent. They elbowed their companions.

"You motherfucker!" Tig screamed. "What do you want?"

The rest of the patrons in the Inn fell silent. As one, they looked at Simon.

Simon smiled. "I have come for you, Tig."

"Where's Sophie? Outside with the rest of the dogs?"

"Sophie is back in Freecourt, where she belongs."

All eyes in the bar travelled from Simon to Tig and back again.

"Get the fuck out!" Tig screamed again. She took a step, transferred one of the tankards of ale to her other hand and threw the other at Simon. Simon dodged the tankard which shattered on the floor where it landed.

"You're paying for that, Tiana," Collin yelled.

Tig advanced on Simon, she took the other tankard and threw that at him as well. He threw up his arm to deflect it. She came toward him, grabbing tankards and glasses, hurling them all at Simon. She came to an older gentleman's table and reached out for his glass. He held up his hand, picked up his glass, drained it, and handed it to Tig. That glass flew at Simon as well.

"I don't want you," Tig spat at Simon and threw another glass at him. "Just fucking leave!"

Simon stood his ground. He had expected this. He had hoped that it would not have happened in front of what seemed to be the whole village. The sight of her had brought a wave of relief that washed over him. She was still here. He had found her. She was the Tig that he loved. He would endure this and more to get her back. "I'm not leaving without you, Tig," he responded.

She screamed with fury and ran at him. Patrons hurriedly backed out of the way, bumping into each other.

Simon stood still, his arms at his sides. He waited until she was within reach.

Tig threw out a fist, aiming for his throat. He caught her fist in his hand. She brought her other fist up, aiming for his chin. He caught that one as well. Forcefully, he pulled her toward him and threw her hands down. He grabbed her upper arm and spun her around, catching her in a bear hug.

Tig began to struggle. She threw her head back, attempting to connect with his head. Simon dodged her.

"Let me go, you fuck," she screamed. Her face was red with fury. She kicked behind her connecting with one of Simon's legs.

He bent his head to her ear. "Stop this Tig. Let me talk to you," he said in a low voice.

Tig was beyond hearing. Simon lifted her off her feet, holding her struggling body against his. He began to back toward the door.

"Let me go, let me go," Tig repeated.

From off to his left, a deep voice said, "She said to let her go." Simon turned to identify the speaker and instead saw a hammer in the shape of a fist come straight for his face.

A powerful blow landed on Simon's cheek. Simon

released Tig and staggered backward into the mass of onlookers, who propped him up. Gilbert jumped in between Simon and his attacker, drawing his sword. Tig ran to the man and put her hand on his arm.

"Sire, are you all right?" Gilbert shouted. People in the bar gasped. This man was a king!

"Mathan, stop," Tig said.

Simon put a hand to his cheek. He took in the sight of Tig with her hand on Mathan's arm. "You have got to be kidding me," he said.

Mathan put his arm around Tig and glared at Simon. Tig looked at him with defiance, jutting her chin out.

Absolute silence reigned in the Inn. Suddenly, Gilbert sheathed his sword and said, "Lady Tig, it has been far too long since I have seen you."

She tore her eyes away from Simon. A smile lit her face. "Grunt, I had not noticed you there." She went to him and embraced him. "I've missed you."

He smiled down at her and took her hand. "Come, tell me what has been happening with you." He pulled her with him, away from Simon and Mathan, toward the bar.

Voices exploded. Mathan and Simon glared at each other. The door to the Inn opened, two men entered followed by a streak of gray, barking and yipping. It was Griffin. He ran straight for Simon, jumping up and licking his face. Simon laughed. He tried to contain the excited dog, but Griffin would have none of that.

"No dogs in the bar," Collin shouted.

Simon went to the door and opened it. "C'mon, Grif, let's cool off," he said as he left.

CHAPTER 17

Tig went home with Mathan that night. He had come to the bar to speak to her, to see if they could work things out. She had asked him if she could spend the night at his cottage and he had happily agreed. She didn't want to see Simon again. The Inn was full, there was nowhere else for Simon to stay. She hoped that he would be gone tomorrow and that would be the last that she saw of him.

The ride to Mathan's cottage had been quiet. Once the horses had been tended to, they sat across from each other over a cup of tea. Mathan asked her about Simon and she told him that she had been his aide-de-camp and military advisor in charge of training his men.

"There must be more to it than that, Tiana. The man has come a great distance looking for you," Mathan stated.

"Yes," was her only response.

"Do you love him, Tiana?"

She responded a moment later, anger tinging her voice, "I did."

Tig refused to answer any more questions or speak any further on the matter of Simon. They went to bed, each lying rigidly on their own side of the mattress.

In the meantime, Simon was trying to make arrangements

with Collin for a room, but all the rooms were taken and would be for the next two nights. After much discussion Collin admitted that there were two more rooms. One was Tiana's room, the other more of a closet that Collin used on the rare nights that he and his wife argued and she refused to let him share their bed.

Simon knew that if he took Tig's room he would be forcing her to return to Mathan's cottage and, most likely, his bed. And so, it was decided that he and Gilbert would share the closet for the next two nights and then they would move into other rooms.

"How long do you intend to stay, Sire?" Collin asked.

"As long as it takes," Simon replied.

"Any idea how long that will be?"

"Knowing Tig…" Simon said as he looked at Gilbert.

"It could be months, Sire," Gilbert responded.

Simon could see the dollar signs rolling through Collin's mind. "Aye, she can be stubborn."

"But worth every second of my time," Simon said as he smiled.

Simon looked forward to the challenge. He knew that Tig would be difficult, but he also knew that, to some extent, he deserved whatever she would do. Deny it as she may, Simon also knew that she still loved him. Only strong emotions would have evoked such a response from her that night. He was betting it was love and not hate.

The next day Tig came in through the kitchen. She grabbed

her apron from the hook by the door and put it on, tying it behind her. "Busy?" she asked the cook.

"Very. You'd best hurry out there," he said.

Tig could hear the voices coming from the bar. There were a fair number of people there. She would be busy, but she needed any tips she could get to help pay for the dishes she broke last night. Too bad she hadn't hit Simon with any of them.

She entered the bar. Every table was taken, every space at the bar occupied. She surveyed the crowd, her eyes going to each table and the number of people seated there. She skimmed over the tables, stopped, and looked at the table in the corner. Gilbert sat there and she beamed a smile at him. Beside him sat Simon. She glared at him.

She turned to Collin. "I am not serving him."

Collin knew who she meant. "You will serve him. He is a paying customer and he is staying here."

"I am not serving him." Tig's voice was raised.

"You are. He is a king. A king in my establishment. You will serve him and you will be happy to do it," Collin replied loudly.

The volume in the Inn lowered. Customers were looking at their meals or into their glasses, but leaning toward the bar to hear every word of their exchange.

"If you are so honored to have him here, perhaps you should serve him," Tig said forcefully.

"It is your job to look after the customers, Tiana, and that is what you will do if you want to continue to work here," Collin yelled at her. "They have placed their order; you can serve it."

Tig glared at Collin. She turned to Simon and shot daggers at him with her eyes. He smiled back at her. In a huff, she stomped into the kitchen.

She picked up two bowls of stew, placed them on plates, and added two thick slices of bread to each plate. She carried them out to Simon's table. She placed one plate in front of Gilbert. "The stew here is very good, Grunt, enjoy!" She slammed the other plate onto the table in front of Simon, almost half the stew sloshed out of the bowl, onto the plate and the table. "You can choke on your lunch," she spat at Simon.

"Tiana!" Collin yelled at her. He and everyone else in the room had heard and seen her treatment of Simon and Gilbert.

Simon glanced at Collin, then looked at Tig and smiled. "Thank you, Tig," he said, "you are most gracious."

Her face turned red with anger. She opened her mouth to respond, thought better of it, and then stormed off.

Tig was busy for the whole day, taking orders, serving food and cleaning tables. She returned to Gilbert several times to see if he wanted another ale while ignoring Simon. In the end, Collin was forced out from behind the bar to tend to Simon, offering his apologies for Tiana's rude behavior. "I would expect nothing else from her. She is a wonder is she not?" Simon said in a voice loud enough to carry to the next table where she was busy clearing it of dishes. His comment only served to infuriate her more. How dare he say something so complimentary? He was still trying to win her over with his honied words when all she wanted was for him to go. If he was expecting any response from her, he was mistaken. She continued on as if she had not heard him, ignoring him, the same as any other clump of dirt on the floor.

When Simon and Gilbert had finished their meal and had their share of ale they walked through the village, visiting the various stands set up for the Fall Fair. News of his arrival and the reason for his visit had spread through the village. Simon received his fair share of bows and winks along with several pats on the arm from elderly women.

Tig spent the night in her room at the Inn. She was up before the sun rose, running and practicing. She finished her workout and returned to her room to change and freshen up. By now morning had arrived and the sun was up. She went to the stable to tend to Juno, giving her some oats and brushing her. Tig finished brushing Juno and turned to put down the brush. A bouquet of flowers appeared before her. They were beautiful. An assortment of bright blooms surrounded by lush greenery. She gasped and reached out for them, then followed the arm that held them and looked into Simon's eyes.

"For you, Tig," he said.

A softness came into her eyes. Simon's heart leapt. A split second later, anger took hold of her.

"Is this what you do when your wife is angry at you, Simon, offer her flowers?"

"I am not married, Tig. I told you that Sophie was gone. I will never see her again."

She grabbed the flowers out of his hand and held them

in front of Juno who, after a brief inspection, took a big bite and began chomping on the blooms. Tig stared at Simon the whole time, daring him to say something.

He smiled at her, a boyish grin. He couldn't help himself, he raised his hand to stroke her cheek. Tig slapped his hand away. "Don't touch me," she said before throwing what was left of the bouquet into Juno's stall and storming off.

Tig walked into the bar. Again, it was full, all tables filled. Again, Simon and Gilbert sat at the table in the corner. Today, however, their meals were in front of them. She turned to look at Collin.

"I can't have you chase off my best customers, Tiana. I will see to them."

"Thank you, Collin," she said before running off to take orders.

It had been a long day. The last for a while, Tig assumed. Today was the last day of the Fall Fair. Tomorrow, lunch might be busy, but most of those from outside the village would be travelling back to their homes. Tig sat outside the Inn, enjoying a peaceful moment, Griffin at her feet. She closed her eyes and immediately Simon's face was before her, his boyish grin, his smiling eyes. It was nice to see him again, to have him near. She wanted so much to be with him but she couldn't. She wouldn't make the mistake of giving her heart to him again.

CHAPTER 18

The next day Tig came in the kitchen, pulled her apron down from its hook and tied it on.

"Thank goodness it's back to normal," she said to the cook.

"Hardly," he replied. "Take a look."

Tig walked into the bar. Every table was filled and the bar was crowded. She looked at all the customers in surprise, noting that they were all locals. She assumed that perhaps they had done good trade at the Fall Fair and were treating themselves to a meal at the Inn. She noted Gilbert and Simon in their usual spot before entering the room and starting her shift.

She was in the kitchen, delivering orders to the cook, when Collin came in. "You have to serve the king today, Tiana. I am too busy to take the time away from the bar. I don't want any arguments from you about it either. Just do it."

The cook put two dishes in front of her. "For the king and his man," he said.

She picked them up and took the plates to Simon and Gilbert. She placed the dishes in front of them, intending to leave immediately. Simon reached out and took her hand.

"Tiana," he said.

Everyone in the bar stopped talking.

"You remind me of someone I know," Simon continued, "she is as beautiful as you, but she is kind and caring, gentle and loving, and when she smiles, she fills my heart."

Oddly, Tig thought she heard a number of people sigh.

"Are those Mrs. Abbot's words?" Tig asked.

Simon smiled. "Mrs. Abbot and I agree to disagree on certain matters."

She glared at Simon and pulled her hand out of his. "Well, then, if you had such tender feelings for this woman, I guess you shouldn't have been planning your wedding to Sophie."

Gasps were heard in the bar. Tig spun around to see who was listening. Everyone avoided her gaze. They were all lifting forks and spoons to their mouths.

She left Simon's table and bustled back into the kitchen to pick up the next orders. She met Simon's eyes on her way into the dining room. He was annoyed at her, she could read it on his face. Good, she thought. If he thought she was going to let him back into her heart, he was in for a hard lesson in reality.

It was a beautiful morning. The sky was blue and the sun was warm. Tig had finished her workout and had tended to Juno. She was sitting on the bench in front of the Inn, basking in the warm rays. Her shift would begin in a few hours and she was hoping it would not be as hectic as it had been for the past week. Not that she minded being busy, it made her day go faster and kept her mind off Simon.

Ah yes, her traitorous mind. Seeing him every day—his smile, his voice when he spoke to her, all of that—was weakening her resolve to stay away from him. She wished he would just leave, go home to Moregane, and leave her alone. But did she really? His room was a short distance down the hall from hers and sometimes, at night, she could feel him there. She knew what he was doing as he prepared to go to bed. She knew that he slept naked. That thought brought a whole other set of images to mind. It took everything she had to not take the few steps needed to reach his door.

She blew out a breath and turned her head. There was a man approaching the Inn, leading a cow, no doubt headed to market. Someone sat down beside her. She continued to watch the man and the cow as they approached.

"What are you thinking?" Simon asked.

Tig jerked at the sound of his voice and turned to look at him.

"My thoughts are none of your concern," she replied.

"They were once. They still are." He picked up her hand.

The man and cow had reached the Inn. He stopped suddenly and began to examine the rope that was tied around the beast's neck.

"You are so charming, Simon."

"Am I?"

"You know you are."

"Charming enough for you, Tig?" He brought her hand to his lips and kissed it.

"Charming enough for the whole fucking world,

Simon, but I know what lies beneath your charm," she said as she pulled her hand away from his, glaring at him.

Out of the corner of her eye, Tig noted that the man was allowing the cow to graze on the grass directly across the road from them.

"Tell me, then, what's beneath my charm? Is it the love that I have for you? The desire that has brought me here in the hopes that I can win you back? Is that what seems to be so annoying to you?"

"You want me back so you can torture me some more. You're here because you seem to think that I belong to you and you want your toy back."

"You don't belong to me, Tig, you belong *with* me, and I belong with you."

"Says you. You think you know everything."

"I don't know everything, Tig, but I do know you. You are mine and I am yours, stop this nonsense and come back to me." He lifted his hand and stroked her cheek. "Please." He leaned toward her and kissed her lightly on the lips.

Tig placed her hands on his chest and shoved him away from her. "No. Stop wasting your time here. Just leave. I'm done with you. You are nothing to me anymore. Go back to Moregane, Simon."

She stood, faced the man across the road, who had stopped all pretense of caring for his cow and was openly watching them. "Seen enough?" she shouted as she walked away from Simon.

She hurried into the kitchen and grabbed her apron from

the hook; she was running a little late.

"Take your time, Tiana, no need to hurry," the cook said.

"Really?"

"Truly, so far it's just Old Ned."

Tig went into the bar. Old Ned was the only customer there. It appeared as if she would have time to do the things that she had been letting go for the past week because she had been too busy to attend to them. She got a bucket of water and a cloth, went outside, and began to wash the windows. Then she washed the windows on the inside.

She got another tankard of ale for Ned and waited on two tables before returning to her tasks. She wiped down the front of the bar, dusted the mantle, swept out the hearth, refilled Ned's tankard, served dessert to one of the tables and wiped down the other table and chairs when those people paid their tab and left.

All that done, she got a glass of water for herself and went to sit with Ned.

He had just finished telling her the story of how he had met his wife, God bless her soul, when he looked at Tig and said, "You're being awfully hard on that man, Tiana."

Tig was caught off guard by his statement. "You don't know the whole story, Ned. He deserves it."

"Aye, maybe he does," Ned agreed, his rheumy eyes fixed on her face, "but no man will beg forgiveness forever. He is not from here; he will admit defeat eventually and leave. Is that what you want?"

She was saved from having to answer that question

when two more people walked in and took a table. She got up to serve them.

Simon and Gilbert had not come for lunch, nor did they appear for supper. Tig did not hear them return that night and, if they did, it was after she had fallen asleep.

The next two days were much the same. Business at the Inn was back to normal and not very busy. Simon and Gilbert had gone on a hunting trip, at Collin's suggestion, and were not expected back for a few days. Tig kept as busy as she could, trying not to think about Simon, or miss him.

On the third day, Tig was in the bar, cleaning tables that had just been vacated when the door opened. Simon and Gilbert walked in. Gilbert held a stringer of pheasant. He greeted her and continued through to the kitchen. Simon looked at her, a smile on his face. "Miss me?" he asked.

Tig felt a smile tug at the corner of her mouth, then got it under control. "Were you gone?"

Simon put a hand up over his heart. "You are a shrew, Tig. You wound me deeply."

"Unfortunately, I think you'll live." She finished wiping down the table and walked toward him, meaning to go into the kitchen.

Simon took her hand as she neared him and brought it to his lips. "I missed you," he whispered to her.

She yanked her hand out of his, pushing past him. She wanted to grab him and drag him upstairs to his room. She wanted to rip the clothes off his body and fuck him until he begged for mercy. He was charming and playful and she had missed him. More than she wanted to admit. He had started playing dirty in this game of wits and she knew that she was going to lose if she didn't harden her heart against him.

The special that night was roast pheasant, courtesy of Simon and Gilbert. It was not uncommon to have roast pheasant at the Inn, they had had it many times in the past, but it did not draw a large crowd because it was also a little more expensive than their usual fare. That night, however, the Inn was packed once again, standing room only at the bar.

Tig was running in and out of the kitchen, filling orders, carrying meals out and bringing dirty dishes back in. Collin was pouring drinks and refilling tankards of ale. It was a madhouse.

Tig was taking a breather in the kitchen, waiting for the cook to fill more plates when Collin yelled for her. "Tiana, two more pheasant dinners!"

She rolled her eyes at the cook. He put down two plates. She picked them up and went into the bar. Collin was waiting for her. "The king and his man," he said, nodding toward Simon's table. She swore under her breath and went to deliver the plates to Simon's table. As she approached his table, all talking ceased, cutlery froze in mid-air, glasses were put down, all eyes turned toward her.

"Your dinners," she said as she placed the dishes before them.

"Thank you, Lady Tig," Gilbert said.

She spun on her heel and turned toward the kitchen. As if a switch had been turned on, voices rose, cutlery scraped against plates, and everyone picked up the conversations that had suddenly stopped. Strange, Tig thought, as she left the bar and entered the kitchen to get more plates.

Dinner orders were winding down, thankfully, as the pheasant was almost all gone. No one seemed to want to leave. Tig was serving more dessert and tea than she had ever done. She noticed that Gilbert and Simon had finished their meals. She went to collect their plates. Silence descended once again.

She reached out to take Simon's plate when he took her hand in his. "You left me when I needed you most, Tig," he said solemnly. He put his other hand over top of hers, looking into her eyes.

She pulled her hand away. "Maybe you shouldn't have been thinking about putting me in jail," she snapped back.

"I did no such thing!"

"No, because you didn't have the chance. I left before you could."

"I would not have ever imprisoned you."

"Tell me, Simon, what did you think when you first saw Sophie's face? What did she tell you? You believed her, I know you did. What were you going to do?"

Tig stood taller as she watched Simon process those questions. He had sent the guards looking for her. He would have punished her if she had been there. She saw those emotions play across his features.

"Do you really think I want to return to you, knowing

what you would have done to me?" she asked, acid dripping from her tongue.

Simon erupted, pushing his chair back against the wall. He leaned over the table and grabbed her upper arm, pulling her face to his. "DAMN IT, TIG, I DIDN'T KNOW WHAT HAD HAPPENED. YOU KNEW THAT! YOU KNEW THAT AND YOU LEFT."

"I told you not to bring her. I warned you and you told me you didn't care what I thought and you did it anyway. After what she did to me, do you think that I would wait around to see what form of punishment she would think of?"

"Give me something, Tig, give me an inch, a thread, anything, to show me that you forgive me and that there is still hope for us."

"I gave you your life when you walked in here. I have nothing else to give you."

Simon put his other hand behind her head. Pulling her toward him he lowered his head to hers and claimed her lips in a savage kiss. He released her. "You have that to give me."

"Don't ever touch me again, Simon, or I swear I will gladly cut your heart out," she spat, a knife pressed under his chin.

Simon froze. He looked into her eyes. He put his hand on hers and pushed the knife away. He spoke to her softly so that only she could hear him. "Is this how we are to end, Tig? Is this what you truly desire?"

"Yes." Tig sheathed her knife. Turning, she strode out of the bar, through the kitchen, and out the door.

• • •

Gilbert watched as Simon straightened up and glared after Tig as she left. Then he walked out the front door.

People in the bar began to breathe again. The noise rose to a crescendo. Gilbert motioned to Collin for an ale. Collin pulled the ale and brought it to him.

"Nothing is ever easy with those two," he said to Collin.

"Do you think he will win her over?" Collin asked.

"This afternoon I would have said yes, no question. Right now, I am not so sure."

CHAPTER 19

The next day the Inn was packed again. Simon and Gilbert sat at their usual table. Tig did not come to work that afternoon or that evening. Juno and Griffin were both gone as well. Collin did not know where they were.

After supper, Gilbert went to the stable. Juno was in her stall, munching on oats. Tig sat on a bale of hay, combing Griffin, who sat at her feet.

"Lady Tig," he greeted her.

Tig did not respond. She remained focused on Griffin.

"We are leaving tomorrow morning."

Still she did not respond.

"Talk to me, Lady Tig. We have always been able to speak to one another."

"I have nothing to say, Grunt."

"Will you not miss us when we go?"

"I will miss you."

"And the king?"

Tig did not respond. How could she? She would miss Simon. When he left, he would be taking a part of her with him, the part of her that he had always had, the part that she had given him from the first time they had met.

Gilbert squatted down in front of her. "He suffers, you

know. He knows what he has done and he is sorry for it. How can you blame him for what he did when he did not even remember who you were?"

"I know he's sorry. I'm sorry too."

"Can't you forgive him?"

"It's not that simple, Grunt, I wish it were."

"It *is* that simple, don't you agree?"

"He hated me. How could he have hated me so much one day and then love me another? Maybe he doesn't love me as much as he thinks he does."

"He does love you, Lady Tig. We are here, are we not? You have led him on a merry chase and he has followed willingly. What more does he have to do?"

"Nothing more, Grunt. I think I have suffered enough at his hands, don't you?"

Now Gilbert was lost for words.

"Well, then, I will bid you good night, Lady Tig, and farewell, though I wish it were not so."

The bar was empty, Collin had gone home to bed, all lights had been extinguished. Tig walked softly up the stairs, past Gilbert's room. A sliver of light shone at the bottom of Simon's door. She crept past it toward her room. She stopped in the hallway, turned, and walked to Simon's door. She lifted the latch and slipped into his room.

His shirt was off. He was facing his bed. He turned when the door opened and watched as Tig stepped in and closed the door behind her. She stood where she was, watching him. She could see he was desperate to run to her and take her in his arms, but he didn't. She would have to make the next move. It would kill him to have to wait, but he would.

She brought her hand up to the door latch, meaning to open it and leave, but she didn't. She let her hand drop back to her side. She walked toward him but stayed outside of his reach. She studied his face, the face that she loved, she read the hope in his eyes. His chest was bare, his pants unbuttoned and hanging low on his hips. She wanted to reach out and touch him.

"You hated me," she said softly. "You were disgusted by me."

"I know."

"I was alone, surrounded by people who didn't like me."

"Yes."

"There was no one to champion me."

"I know that too."

"You couldn't even remember my name." Simon winced at the pain in her words.

"Your name is written in my heart, Tig."

"I had to leave. You brought Sophie back. You were going to punish me."

"I didn't know." He took a step toward her. Tig did not move. He lifted his hand and stroked her cheek. "Let me make it up to you, Tig, for the rest of my life."

He put both his hands on her shoulders and pulled her toward him. She went willingly into his arms. He bent and kissed her forehead, stroking her hair. "I'm sorry," he said as he hugged her, "so, so sorry."

She lifted her face to his. He kissed her softly, running his hands down her back. She wrapped her arms around his neck. He deepened his kiss and pulled her up against him, lifting her feet off the ground. The want built in both of them, their kissing became feverish. Simon released her, letting her slide down his body. He took a deep breath.

Tig began ripping at the laces of her dress. Simon took her hands in his and kissed them. He released her hands and reached for the laces, pulling them free, loosening her bodice. He slid her dress off her shoulders, pushing it past her hips and letting it fall on the floor. Next, he undid the tie to her shift, pulling it open, letting it slide off her body to join her dress on the floor. She stood naked before him. Simon's eyes travelled down her body, from her eyes, to her lips, her shoulders, her breasts, her hips, her mound, her legs, and her feet.

He pulled her to him again, her breasts pressing against his chest, his hands running down her body to cup her ass in his hands. Tig was panting from want. She stepped back from him and slid his pants over his hips. He was magnificent, his erection evidence of his desire for her. She reached her hand toward him, but he caught it and put it on his shoulder. He bent down and scooped her up in his arms carrying her the few feet to the bed where he gently laid her down.

He lay beside her, his hand cupping her breast, pinching her nipple, then travelling down to her stomach, over her mound and in between her legs. She was wet for him. He bent his head and kissed her slowly, longingly, his fingers finding her nub, swirling around it. Tig gasped from the sensation.

He continued his ministrations, staring into her eyes before kissing her neck, then her shoulder. He licked her nipple then took it between his teeth. She moaned. He slid his fingers into her, kissing and licking her body down to the source of her need. He lifted her leg and placed it on his shoulder. He looked deep into her eyes again then dipped his head. He licked the moist folds of her mound, finding her opening and inserting his tongue. He flicked her nub with his tongue and then thrust it into her again.

Tig's hands were wrapped in his hair, pushing his face into her pussy, moaning from the sensations that ran through her. She pulled his head up. Her lips were parted and moist, her eyes half closed and glazed with desire. She pulled him again, forcing him up toward her face. She let go of his hair and took his face in her hands. She lifted herself up, taking his lips in a searing kiss.

She gave into the pleasure coursing through her body. Only Simon could make her feel like this. She hated herself for her weakness, for giving herself to Simon, when she was so angry at him. She allowed him to touch her like only he could and she touched him too, stroking all the parts of his body that she loved, that were so familiar to her, but she refused to release the iron hold on her heart. She would give him her body, but not her heart.

"Do it," she panted, "please."

He moved his body in between her legs. Slowly he slid

into her, watching the ecstasy written on her face. He began to move. He would savor every minute of this, the response of her body to his touch, the look of desire on her face. He stroked slowly but powerfully, jolting her body with every thrust. Tig dug her nails into his shoulders, her head thrown back, her body arching to meet him. There was always this between them, the language that did not require words, the give and take that surmounted anger and guilt. He would use it to his advantage tonight. He would win her back.

She was nearing the edge, he could feel it, and he was there too. He stopped his movements and took her lips again, kissing her sweetly. He stayed in her, waiting for the tension in her body to ease, before pushing into her again.

He brought her to the edge of climax again and again, always to the edge, then stopping and waiting for her to relax before beginning again. He made love to her for what seemed like hours, worshipping her body, showering her with kisses, whispering words of love. Tig was in a haze of pleasure, her eyes half closed, her lips pressed firmly together, her body molding to his. Finally, Simon brought her to the edge of climax and took her over it. Her body tensed. She wrapped herself around him as she came. He pushed into her one last time then allowed himself his release.

He stayed in her as he held her and fell to his side. He wrapped his arms around her holding her trembling body and whispering softly in her ear. When she let him go, Simon leaned over her, brushing her hair from her face and kissing her gently. He lifted the blankets over them. She rolled onto her side. Simon spooned her, holding her tightly to him before falling into a deep sleep.

Simon woke to the sound of Gilbert pounding on his door. "Sire, are you awake?"

He moaned. "Yes, yes. Just a moment." He sat up, placing his feet on the floor. Tig would have to get up as well. They would be leaving shortly. He reached behind him, then turned when he felt nothing but the mattress and twisted sheets. She was not there.

Of course, she was nothing if not dedicated to her fitness. He glanced out the window, the sun had risen; she would have been done by now, he thought. She must be packing her things, was his next thought.

He rose and pulled on his pants.

"Are you awake, Sire?" Gilbert called from the other side of the door.

"Yes," he said. He picked up his shirt and walked to the door of his room, opening it, and allowing Gilbert to enter.

"All is ready. The horses are saddled. I have purchased some food and packed that as well. Some breakfast and we shall be on our way."

Simon pulled on his shirt, walked past Gilbert, down the hall to Tig's room and opened the door. She was not there either. Her clothes and accessories were in their places. Nothing was packed. He swore and returned to his room. "I'll meet you downstairs," he said to Gilbert. He finished dressing and packing then headed downstairs.

Collin was placing two plates on their table when he entered the bar. "Where is Tig?" he asked.

Collin shrugged his shoulders. "I have not seen her this morning," he said and walked away.

Ignoring the meal, Simon went outside to the stable. Juno was gone. He whistled for Griffin, but the dog did not appear. He stood for a moment as it dawned on him that Tig was gone, avoiding him, not intending to return to Moregane with him. Last night had been her farewell to him.

CHAPTER 20

Tig sat in the copse of trees at Mathan's farm. She was waiting for time to pass. She would sit there until it was time for her to leave for her shift at the Inn. Simon would be gone by then for sure. She didn't want to face him, to tell him that she was not going to Moregane and then argue with him about it. She would have been in danger of giving in to his demand that she return with him.

She thought back on last night, on his words of apology. What was she doing here? She wavered between her resolve to stay and her desire to go with Simon. He was sorry, he swore it, and she believed him, but full forgiveness was not in her heart.

She was a fighter who would fight to death, but the wounds he had inflicted on her were deep and festering. What would her future with Simon be? There was an undeniable chemistry between them. Even when he did not know who she was, he had felt it. But, apparently for him, that was not enough. Twice he had brought Sophie to Moregane despite the fact that she was there. Was that her ultimate fate, to be Simon's whore while he courted and married another noblewoman to be his Queen? She had no doubt that Sophie was no longer in his life and never would be again. It had never occurred to her before that her lack of noble breeding was a negative in Simon's eyes and because of that she would never be enough for him.

But the fire between them, the arguing, the passion, would that last forever? At times he infuriated her like no one had ever done before. She would have gladly killed him over and over again during the past five years she had known him, but the way he made her feel, in bed and out of it, when they were on good terms, was also something she had never felt with anyone else. She had not been some naive schoolgirl when she met him, she had had her share of men, and she knew that what they shared was rare. But was it sustainable? Outside of Simon and Gilbert she had no friends or allies in this world. Most of the castle staff feared her and Mrs. Abbot outright hated her.

She had made a life for herself here. People liked her. Old Ned wanted to marry her, not that she would ever consider it. She was an independent woman in a world where that did not exist. If she were to stay here, she would always have a home. She could always take a lover to sate her desires. Who knows, maybe one day she would marry and have children.

She shook her head at that last thought and then realized it was time for her to go.

She came in through the kitchen and pulled her apron down from its hook. "Busy?" she asked the cook.

He nodded his head toward the bar. "Take a look yourself."

Tying her apron behind her she walked down the short

hallway into the bar. It was packed and sitting at the corner table, leaning back in his chair with his arms crossed, was Simon. He was furious. He glared at her when he saw her. "Tig," he bellowed.

She spun around, intending to return to the kitchen. Collin stepped in front of her blocking her exit. "You have customers to serve," he said.

"Tig," Simon called again.

She turned back toward the bar, walked into the aisle, toward the front door.

"Don't you take another step," Simon threatened her.

She stopped dead in her tracks. Simon had never spoken to her in that tone of voice before, even when he did not remember who she was. The front door opened and Gilbert walked in.

"Gilbert," Simon called.

Gilbert looked toward him, nodded his head and approached Tig.

"Lady Tig, I am placing you under arrest," he said as he took her hand and slipped a loop of rope over her wrist.

"For what," she demanded.

"Horse theft and theft of livestock," he responded taking her other hand and looping the rope around her wrist.

"Theft of livestock? What livestock?" she said.

Simon stood; she heard him approach her from behind. "The evidence," he called. The door opened and Old Ned entered, leading Griffin on a short length of rope.

"Juno is my horse. She has always been my horse. Griffin followed me. I didn't steal him," she stated.

Gilbert looked behind her to Simon. "You will be returned to Moregane to face justice, Lady Tig."

"This is a joke, surely," she sputtered. "And you," she glared at Old Ned, "you traitor."

He shrugged sheepishly.

Simon moved to stand in front of her. He was still angry. "You—" he couldn't finish his sentence. Instead, he grabbed the rope binding her wrists and pulled her toward him.

Tig pulled back, resisting him. "I am not going with you."

"You are."

She yanked on her wrists, "I am not."

"You are, and you are coming now." He hauled her toward him, pulling her off balance, into his chest.

"Simon," she said, "you are so strong!" She tilted her head back and looked into his eyes, a smile on her lips.

His eyes narrowed, suspicious at what she was up to.

"Untie me, please." She batted her eyes at him. She leaned against him, pushing her breasts into his chest. "I will come with you willingly." She lifted her face to his, inviting a kiss. "I concede. You have won me back."

He lowered his face to hers and kissed her. He released her hands, took her in his arms and kissed her deeply. He put his forehead on hers, gazing into her eyes. "No."

"You bastard!" Tig pushed herself away from him. "I am not going with you. You can't—"

"I can and I will," he said as he took her bound wrists in his hand again. He turned and pulled her behind him, out the door of the Inn.

Their horses were there, Juno was laden with packs. Gilbert was already mounted, waiting for them.

Behind them, the people who had been in the bar were streaming out, lining up in front of the Inn.

Simon pulled her along behind him, past Juno, to his horse. He turned, grabbed her around the waist, and lifted her off the ground. She put her foot out, into the stirrup, and mounted his horse. She reached for the reins, but Simon grabbed them away from her. He pulled her foot out of the stirrup and mounted, sitting behind her.

"I can ride my own horse," she said. "I am not riding with you."

"No, you can't and yes, you are," he stated. "I know what you can do on a horse and you will not be given that opportunity."

She began to wriggle, trying to slide away from him and off the horse.

"That is quite pleasant, Tig," he whispered into her ear, nuzzling her neck. "Don't stop."

"Fuck you," she spat.

"I hope so." He took the reins in one hand and with the other he snugged her tightly up against him. He looked at Gilbert and nodded. Leading Juno, Gilbert turned his horse toward the road and left. Simon turned his horse and followed behind them. Griffin, who had been lounging in the dirt, barked happily, lunged to his feet and ran after them. Within minutes they had left the village and were into the forest on their way back to Moregane.

Tig sat in stony silence, furious at this turn of events.

Simon, his anger dissipated, was happy. They were headed back to Moregane and Tig was with them. He would have preferred that she come willingly, but this would work too. They would be on the road for months. Certainly, her resolve would weaken, she wouldn't be angry at him the whole way. She did love him, he knew it. Somewhere along the way, he would win her over. How, he hadn't quite worked out yet, but he would.

CHAPTER 21

If nothing else, Tig was stubborn. She refused to speak to Simon unless it was absolutely necessary, and, for once, her anger included Gilbert, whom she refused to speak to at all. Even Juno seemed to be out of sorts, having been relegated to acting as a pack horse. The only one of Tig's party who seem unaffected by this change of events was Griffin. He was happy to be on the road again and happy to be with all the people he loved.

Tig was never left alone, never afforded any privacy, even during their rest stops she was forced to remain within sight of Simon who would discreetly turn his back on her, but, only for so long. When their gazes met, her eyes would narrow and she would hastily look away.

Only during the evening, when supper was done, would she break her silence. She would sit with Griffin and speak to him in low, soothing tones, petting him and rubbing his massive belly. Then, she would curl up with him and together they would fall asleep.

The only moments she had to herself were in the early morning when she awoke and Simon and Gilbert slept. She would work at the knots in the rope binding her wrists, hoping to loosen them. Every morning Simon would check her bonds, tightening them if required, while looking at her.

He knew she was trying to free herself, but he said nothing to her about it.

Simon was happy but frustrated, she felt it. Her silence was evidence of how angry she was with him though. He would smile at her, hoping to get a favorable response and she would look away. He would reach out to touch her, stroke her cheek or kiss her forehead and she would push him away. The only time she would allow him to touch her was when they were on the horse and he would adjust their bodies so they were comfortable.

Tig's resolve was beginning to fade. She had been furious when she had been bound and forced to travel with Simon. Even Gilbert, whom she thought was her friend, had participated in this farce and was helping Simon hold her captive. But Simon could always find a way through her anger and into her good graces. Even after all the time she spent with him, she didn't know how he did it. Every time he used a different tactic, he would say something, do something or look at her in a certain way and her displeasure would crumble. She was defenseless against his charm.

They were into their second week of travel and were camped off the road. The embers of the fire were dying. Tig was asleep, Griffin stretched out beside her. Gilbert was preparing his bed for the night. Simon stood and went to sit beside Griffin. He reached out and began to stroke the large dog. Griffin groaned, his tail began to thump on the forest floor.

Simon leaned forward and in a low voice asked, "Who's a good boy?"

Griffin, rolled over onto his back, allowing Simon to scratch his belly. "You're a good boy, Griffin," he said as he scratched the beast's massive chest. Griffin stretched his legs over his head, rolled once more until he was lying on his chest. Simon pulled a small piece of meat from his pocket. He held it to Griffin's nose and then threw it a few feet away from him. Griffin jumped up and ran after it, found it, and gobbled it up. Simon slid into the spot that Griffin had occupied. Griffin looked at Simon, wagging his tail, and cocked his head to the side. "Lie down, Griffin," Simon commanded him. Griffin obeyed him immediately.

Simon smiled. No dog was going to take his rightful place. He stretched out beside Tig and covered them both with his blanket.

Tig was warm and comfortable. She drifted slowly toward wakefulness. She felt so relaxed. She could not remember the last time she had felt this at ease. She lay on her side, her arms pulled up to her chest, her face pressed to Griffin's shirt... Her eyes flew open. She was in Simon's arms, her head in the hollow of his neck, her leg thrown over his. Simon held her against him, his arm around her waist, his chin resting on the crown of her head. His breathing was deep and even.

Tig closed her eyes again, enjoying this moment with Simon, the smell of him, the feel of him wrapped around her. How many mornings had she woken in this manner,

Simon naked beside her? How many times had they made love in the sun's first rays streaming into the room and over their bodies? Countless times. But that was then, this was now.

Tig carefully rolled onto her back and then onto her other side. Simon mumbled something in his sleep and pulled her into him. Tig's arms were free. She began to work her wrists, trying to stretch the rope that bound them. She pulled the knot up to her mouth and began to tug at the ends with her teeth. She then scraped it on the ground, trying to loosen it.

"Are you trying to get away?" Simon whispered in her ear.

She ceased her manipulations and lay still.

Simon pulled her closer, his breath on her neck, blowing into her ear. He nuzzled her. "Why don't you stay?" he asked huskily.

She wriggled out of his grasp, laying on her back beside him. He propped himself up on his elbow, looking down at her. He reached up with his other hand, brushing the hair out of her face, looking into her eyes. He leaned forward and kissed her lightly on the lips.

Tig felt desire spring to life in her belly. She accepted Simon's kiss and returned his gaze, lust in her eyes.

Simon saw the request there. He pushed her legs apart and moved between them. He leaned down with a more demanding kiss. He took her bound wrists and held them above her head. Tig lifted one of her legs and rested it on Simon's hips, pushing her pelvis into his. He slipped his tongue into her mouth and Tig welcomed him there.

There was a sudden yelp, Griffin was at their side, worming his way in between them, licking Simon and then Tig. She laughed. He groaned and rolled away from Tig. "Maybe you're not such a good boy after all, Griffin," he said.

Gilbert stirred. He sat up, looking across the fire at the three of them: Simon grimacing, Tig smiling, and Griffin taking playful jumps at the two of them. He threw back his head and laughed.

Gilbert was riding behind Tig and Simon, enjoying the day. The tension that had been with them over the past two weeks had dissipated. There was a more companionable atmosphere among them as they continued on their way.

There was a glint of sunlight on metal on the road ahead of them. They slowed their pace. Gilbert moved his horse in front of Simon and Tig. Griffin became alert, his ears perked forward, his nose lifted into the air. He growled as he trotted beside them. It was not long before a group of six soldiers on horseback materialized, heading in their direction. One of the soldiers pulled ahead of the others, raising his hand to slow the others.

All riders stopped, the lead soldier advancing toward Gilbert.

"Good day," the soldier called.

Gilbert nodded his head in greeting.

The soldier stopped his horse beside Gilbert's. He studied Juno, then Tig, with her bound wrists, and Simon riding behind her. "I am Terrance, a soldier in the service of the Earl of Becksley," he said to Gilbert.

"Gilbert, emissary of Simon Lassiter, King of Moregane."

"And your companions?"

"An officer escorting a prisoner back to Moregane for trial."

Terrance scrutinized Tig and Simon again. "The Earl has heard rumors of the king and his man travelling through our country. He has asked that I extend an invitation to visit. We will be most pleased to escort you, Your Majesty," he said, looking at Simon and bowing his head.

"We would be pleased to accept the Earl's invitation," Simon responded.

Terrance looked back toward his men and raised his hand, making a circular motion. Four of his men rode behind Simon and Tig and turned their horses. Terrance turned his horse around, riding abreast of Gilbert. The remaining solider turned his horse as well and urged it forward, leading the way.

"You are far from home, sir," Terrance said to Gilbert.

"Yes, we are."

"It is odd that just you and your king have travelled alone to capture this woman."

"I suppose it is, but we had to travel fast when we learned of her location. We had no guarantee that she would stay where she was."

"What is her crime? She certainly does not look dangerous."

"Looks are deceiving, are they not? She is perhaps the most dangerous woman you will ever meet."

Terrance raised his eyebrows. "Is she really?"

Gilbert nodded his head. "How long have you served the Earl?"

"Ten years now."

"Is he a reasonable master?"

"Aye. A widower now, not so much piss and vinegar as he once had. I imagine his three daughters have had a hand in softening him."

"You are quite isolated if the Earl has a residence out here."

"A summer estate, four days from the City, but he is still grieving the loss of his wife. It will be a welcome diversion for him to entertain you and your master."

CHAPTER 22

They rode for several hours, turning off the main road, travelling through more forest, over a hill, and into a valley. A large estate sat in the center of the valley, with manicured lawns and a gravel road leading them to the front steps.

The party dismounted. Simon helped Tig down from the horse and put his hand on the rope binding her wrists. Terrance bowed to him. "We will take command of the prisoner, Sire. We have cells to house her during your stay." His eyes had strayed to her face when making the offer to Simon. Tig glared at him with anger and made a move as if to confront him, but was stopped by the king's hand on her bounds.

"She will stay with us," Simon said.

Terrance bowed again. "As you say. If you will follow me." He led them up the stairs and into the mansion.

A servant was waiting for them at the door. "If you will follow me," he said as he led them up another set of stairs and into a sitting room. A fire was burning in the hearth, sofas and chairs were placed in conversation groups. The walls were hung with portraits and landscape paintings. "The Earl will join you momentarily," the servant said as he turned and left the room.

"This is a pleasant surprise, is it not?" Simon said.

"Do you know him, Sire?" Gilbert asked.

"No, but it will be nice to have a bath and a meal, to sleep in a bed for a night or two."

At that moment the Earl entered the room. He was an older gentleman, gray hair, turning to silver, a bit of extra weight around the middle. He wore a smile on his face, but the smile did not reach his eyes. He was dressed in black, the color of mourning.

"Welcome, welcome," he said, his arms spread wide. "How kind of you to accept my invitation." He stopped in front of Simon and bowed. "Sire, Peter Cornish, Earl of Becksley."

"Simon Lassiter, King of Moregane." Simon nodded. "My emissary, Gilbert Lassiter," he said as he indicated Gilbert, "and Lady Tig."

The Earl bowed to Gilbert and turned to Tig. Taking her hand in his, he raised it to his lips and saw the rope binding her wrists. He paused and looked at Simon.

"Lady Tig is my prisoner. We are taking her to Moregane for trial," he explained.

The Earl looked sharply at Tig, then smiled and bent to kiss her hand. "No doubt Terrance told you that we have cells to house criminals. I would be happy to hold her there during your stay."

"Thank you for the offer, but she will stay with me."

"I have many rooms in this estate. We could lock her in a room, give you a chance to let down your guard and relax," the Earl offered again.

Simon looked down at Tig. There was a look of obstinance on her face. He knew she was annoyed that she was being spoken of as if she were not there. He would not have her put in a cell but he couldn't trust her locked in a room either. "Thank you again, Sir, she will stay with me."

"Fine, as you wish. My valet will show you to your rooms. I am sure you will welcome a bath and time to rest. Please join me for supper. We can make plans then."

"Thank you for your hospitality. I look forward to our meal."

Simon and Gilbert were placed in lavish rooms across the hall from one another. When Simon and Tig entered their room, a tub was already sitting in front of the fire that had been lit in the hearth. Moments after the door closed, there was a knock. Simon answered the door and stood aside. A line of servants entered, carrying pails of steaming water that they poured into the tub before filing out and closing the door behind them.

Simon pulled off his jacket and lifted his shirt off. He stood bare-chested as he looked at Tig. "You can bathe first," he said.

She returned his look and held up her hands. "It's going to be difficult bathing while I am tied up."

"Difficult for you," he said with a smirk, "but pleasurable for me."

That was it, that was the phrase, the look, that brought her resolve crumbling into a heap at her feet. She laughed. "You are such a lech!"

"A lech for you, Tig," he said as he walked toward her. He took her bound hands in his and bent to kiss her. "You must promise me you will behave."

"You don't like it when I behave."

He leered at her. "So true."

She squealed at the look on his face. "Is that a promise, Sire?"

"Indeed." He licked his lips.

She giggled and pushed him away. "You are awful."

"But charming." He winked at her.

"Very."

Simon took her hands in his again. "If you try to escape Tig, you will find yourself in a cell," he said seriously, "and if you do manage to get away, I will find you." He began to work at the knot, untying her wrists. "I order you to behave, Tig. Obey your king…for once."

Simon untied the knot and unwound the rope that bound her wrists, dropping it on the floor.

Tig undressed and stepped into the tub. She slid down and let the warm water cover her. She sighed and closed her eyes. Simon knelt beside the tub. He picked up a bar of soap, dipped it in the water and began to lather his hands in suds. Tig sat up and leaned forward. Simon's hands glided down her back and up, over her shoulders. She leaned back allowing Simon's soapy hands to slide down to her breasts, massaging them and tweaking her nipples.

He stood and held out his hand to her. She took his hand and stood. He picked up the soap and lathered his hands again. He moved to stand behind her. He ran his hands down her back to her ass and down her legs. He brought his hands up and slid them between her cheeks, in between her legs.

He came to stand in front of her again. He rubbed her

belly, down to her mound, and in between her legs again. He was pulling his hand out when Tig reached down and grabbed his wrist, halting his withdrawal. She began to sway on his hand, rubbing herself against his fingers and wrist.

He smiled and kissed her gently on the lips. Withdrawing his hand, he undid his pants and let them fall to the floor. He stepped into the tub and pulled Tig against him. He reached down and lifted her leg, grinding against her. She could feel his erection. She grabbed his shoulders and wrapped her other leg around his waist. Simon held her with his arm around her waist. With his other hand he guided himself into her and began to pump hard and fast.

All thought left his head as he slid in and out of her. It was just the feeling of his cock gliding into her soft wetness that existed. He ground his teeth with the need to climax. "Come with me, Tig," he whispered, "I can't wait for you." Her breasts pressed against his chest, her ass in his hands, and his cock plunging in and out of her, that was all that existed for him. He closed his eyes and threw back his head, relishing in the sensations.

"Fuck me hard, Simon," Tig breathed. She nipped at his lobe and slid her tongue into his ear.

Simon groaned. He released Tig. He pulled himself out of her, then turned her around, bent her forward, and slammed his cock into her pussy from behind. Tig braced herself with her hands gripping the edge of the tub. He grabbed her breasts, finding her nipples and pinching them mercilessly hard. A jolt ran from her nipples down to her cunt. Tig screamed, demanding more. Simon continued to slam into her, pushing her forward with each thrust, twisting her nipples.

The pressure in his cock was building. He was going to come; he couldn't hold himself back. With a roar he released her nipples and grabbed her hips, holding her while he pushed himself deep into her. Tig pushed her ass back onto him as he withdrew, then he slammed into her again and came. He fell forward onto her back, holding her still as his cock continued to throb and spew his seed.

At last he stood, pulling her up with him. He nuzzled her neck and wrapped his arms around her. She was his match in every way. No one else could ever take her place. He would never stop wanting her. "I love you," he said.

She pulled away from him and carefully turned around within the limited confines of the tub until she faced him. She smiled and lifted her face toward his, asking for a kiss. He smiled back at her and obliged.

He bent down, picked up a cloth, wet it, and began to wipe the soap off her body. She stood still. He dipped the cloth again, brought it to her chest and wrung it out, letting the water cascade over her breasts. He bent down and licked the still tender buds there, bringing them to attention once more.

"Simon, the water is getting cold," Tig said, pushing his face away from her breasts.

Simon sighed. If they were at Moregane they could have continued to play for hours, but they were not. He finished rinsing her off. She took the cloth from his hand and washed him. Together, they stepped out of the tub and ran for the bed, jumping in and pulling the covers over them. Simon pulled her toward him. She fit against him, snuggled into his chest, his chin resting on the crown of her head.

A knock at the door woke them an hour later. "Dinner will be served in thirty minutes," a voice called from the other side. A moment later they heard the knock on Gilbert's door with the same announcement repeated.

Simon lay on his back, Tig up against him. He sat up and swung his feet onto the floor. He looked over his shoulder at Tig. Her hair was messy, her eyes still clouded by sleep, a half-smile on her lips. What he wouldn't give to be able to slide back into bed with her.

He could tell Tig felt the same. She looked into Simon's eyes, pulled the blankets off her body, and lay there, on display for his hungry eyes. She parted her legs and when he met her eyes, she licked her lips.

"I would if I could, Tig, but we don't have time," he said as he stood and walked away from her. He began to dress and heard her slide out of bed and pad toward the pile of her clothes.

They met Gilbert in the hallway and together they descended to the dining room. The Earl was there with three young women. "Your Majesty, let me introduce my daughters," he said as he bowed. "My eldest, Mary; Constance, the middle one; and my youngest, Fliss."

Simon and Gilbert bowed to the ladies. Tig curtsied. Simon watched as the Earl's attention slid to Tig's wrists and noticed they were no longer bound, but he made no mention of that.

The ladies were all attractive and well dressed. Simon felt Mary's eyes devour him, it was not the first time he had been the object of a woman's attention. He smiled at her and turned his attention to Tig. He noticed a look of annoyance on her face and felt a perverse thrill that she was jealous. At the other end of the line, Fliss had turned a deep scarlet, her eyes cast down to the floor. She peeked up at Gilbert, who was speaking to Constance. A dreamy look came across her face.

The Earl escorted them to the table. Simon sat beside Mary, who sat next to Fliss. Tig sat across from Mary, beside Constance, who sat next to Gilbert. The Earl sat at the head of the table.

Bowls of soup were placed in front of them.

"Moregane," Mary said, "I have heard that name and just recently too."

"I would be surprised if you have heard of our country, Lady Mary," Simon said. "We are some distance away. We do not do any trade or commerce with you or your northern neighbors."

"We are not so cut off from civilization here," the Earl said.

"Moregane, Moregane," Mary repeated. "Oh yes, I remember now." She turned to look at Simon. "You have a demon in your employ, do you not?"

Simon jerked at that statement. Out of the corner of his eye, he saw Tig straighten and tense in her chair.

Gilbert's eyes shot to Tig. Fliss continued to stare at Gilbert.

"Mary," the Earl admonished her.

"'Tis true, father, I have heard the men speak of it. You have a demon that trains your army. Is that not correct?"

Mary, the Earl, and Constance were all looking at Simon, waiting for an answer. "That is correct," he responded, "in a sense."

"Is it gruesome?" Mary asked. "I imagine it is quite bloodthirsty as well. Have you lost many men to its appetite?" There was a gleeful look of anticipation in Mary's eyes. She placed her hand on Simon's arm and leaned toward him. "Do tell us all."

"She is a woman…" Simon began.

"A woman," the Earl exclaimed.

"She is a victim of circumstances, but by no means a victim." Simon looked across the table at Tig. "She is, in reality, kind and caring."

"But she must be a bloodthirsty killer to have earned that name," Mary pressed.

"No," Simon responded. "She is a skilled fighter. I am lucky to have her." Simon was looking directly into Tig's eyes.

"I have heard that the bodies she has left in her wake are countless," Mary said.

"Perhaps we can speak of something else," Simon said to Mary, turning toward her and forcing a smile.

"Of course," she replied, a sly smile tugging at her lips. "You were to marry the Duchess of Chrissley, were you not? Twice?"

The Earl gasped. "Mary!"

Tig stood. "If you will excuse me," she said as she put her napkin on the table, "I feel the need for some air."

Simon looked at Gilbert and nodded. Gilbert stood, pulled Tig's chair out, and took her arm. "I will accompany you Lady Tig," he said.

She nodded her head and they left the dining room. Fliss turned in her chair to watch them walk away.

Simon turned to Mary. "If your intention is to make me feel awkward or uncomfortable, I do not." His eyes went to the Earl and then back to Mary. "I would say that I am leaning toward anger at your impertinence in bringing up such personal matters that are no concern of yours."

Mary blushed. She removed her hand from Simon's arm.

"Ha," the Earl exclaimed. "I have warned you that you would be put in your rightful place one day, Mary, and I believe that day has come." He looked at Simon. "I do apologize for my daughter's behavior Sire. Please do not let this spoil your stay. I welcome you to stay for a week or more. I would welcome the company of a man; I have heard too much of dresses and parties. I need to speak to someone of hunting and fishing."

Simon laughed at that statement. "I would be pleased to stay and share some masculine pursuits with you. What type of fishing do you have here?"

Outside, Tig and Gilbert walked through the garden in companionable silence. It was dusk, the temperature pleasant. Staff had been through the garden, lighting torches to illuminate the pathway.

"I will never be rid of them, Grunt." Tig broke the silence between them.

"Who? Mary and the Earl?"

"No. The Demon and Sophie. They will haunt me forever."

"We all have our burdens in life, Lady Tig. We either shoulder them or give in to them."

"When did you become such a wise young man? I always remember the first time we met—"

"The first time you tried to kill me—"

"I was not going to kill you!"

"You could have fooled me, I almost pissed myself."

They both laughed, and continued to reminisce about those days. They returned to the dining room in time for dessert. When the meal was done the Earl, Simon, and Gilbert went to the study for cigars and liquor while the ladies headed for the sitting room and some card games.

Tig tactfully excused herself feigning a headache, returning to the room she shared with Simon. She stripped and slid back under the covers, quickly falling asleep.

CHAPTER 23

Tig woke the next morning wrapped in the blankets and Simon. She lay on her stomach with Simon covering half of her body with his. She tried to slide out from under him as quietly as she could but her movements woke him. He opened his eyes and rolled onto his back. He put his arm out, hooked Tig, and pulled her to him in a hug. He kissed her forehead and rubbed her back.

"What I would give to stay in bed with you, Tig," he said as he released her and sat up. "But I have a fishing appointment with the Earl this morning."

"I am so out of shape. I haven't had a run in weeks. While you're fishing, I'm going to take Juno for a ride. I hope to find a suitable place for a run and some exercises."

"You will come back?"

"I was planning to."

Simon released the breath that he had been holding. He buttoned his pants, slid on his shirt, and came to the bed. He bent over and kissed Tig on the lips. "Good." He sat and pulled on his boots. He stood, grabbed his jacket, and walked out the door.

Tig lazed in bed before rising and dressing. She went downstairs to find Fliss sitting in the dining room. "May I join you?" she asked as she entered.

"Certainly, Lady Tig."

Tig sat across from Fliss. She guessed that Fliss was seventeen. She was tall and a bit gangly, with the promise of stunning beauty in the next year or two. She was reading a book. "I'm just going to finish this paragraph, if you don't mind," she said.

"Take your time, Fliss. You do not need to entertain me."

A servant entered the room and took Tig's breakfast order.

Fliss picked up a piece of ribbon that was laying on the table, put it in the book, and closed it. She looked across the table at Tig. "Did you sleep well, Lady Tig?"

"I did, thank you."

"Is it true that you are a prisoner?" She took a bite of toast, watching Tig's face.

The servant returned, carrying a plate with eggs, toast, and ham. She placed it in front of Tig and left the room.

Tig looked across the table at Fliss. She did not detect any malice in the girl's question. "It was true. I'm not so sure it still is." She watched Fliss process her response and, anticipating further questions, she added, "It's a long story, Fliss."

Fliss recognized Tig's last statement as a request not to pursue the matter. She shrugged her shoulders. "Do you have plans for today?"

"Lady Tig, you are awake," Gilbert said as he entered the dining room. He came to sit beside her. Tig noticed that Fliss turned a bright red and froze where she sat.

"I am awake, Gilbert, good morning to you."

The servant must have been standing outside the door in the hall to the kitchen. She returned immediately to take Gilbert's breakfast order.

"What are you doing today?" Gilbert asked as he poured a cup of tea for Tig and himself. Using the tongs, he deposited two lumps of sugar in his cup and one in Tig's. He then picked up the cream and poured some into his tea before putting it down and looking at her.

"I was just about to tell Fliss," Tig nodded her head across the table at Fliss, "that I am going to find Juno and go for ride."

"Lady Fliss, I had not noticed you there," Gilbert said. "Good morning to you."

Fliss turned an even darker shade of red. "Thank you, sir, and good morning to you as well." She forced herself to look into his eyes before looking away. Gilbert looked at Tig and smirked.

"I will accompany you, Lady Tig," he stated.

"That will not be necessary, but I would appreciate your company." Tig met his eyes and then shifted her gaze across the table at Fliss and back to his. She raised her eyebrows.

The servant entered carrying Gilbert's breakfast plate. She placed it on the table in front of him and left. Gilbert cleared his throat. "What are you reading, Fliss?"

She started and put her hand on the book. "I…it's…my father…" she was flustered. "It's nothing, really, just something to pass the time. Do you enjoy reading, sir?"

"You may call me Gilbert, madam, and, yes, I do enjoy reading. Sadly, though, I find very little time to do so."

"Of course. Of course, you must be very busy all the time."

"Not all the time, but there are other ways I would prefer to spend my leisure time." There was a wicked tone to his response. Tig kicked him under the table.

Fliss quickly stood. "I should…" she was searching for an excuse, "go." Fliss curtsied and left.

"You are so bad, Grunt," Tig admonished him.

"What? I didn't do anything."

"Men! I hoped you would not be one."

"But I am, Lady Tig, can't help it," he smirked at her.

Tig laughed. "Yes, you are, aren't you?"

Tig ran as if the devil was chasing her. She was panting, pushing herself to her limit. The terrain was unfamiliar to her, which made her flight a bit risky, but she didn't care. It had been weeks since she had had a run. It felt good to stretch her legs and get her blood pumping. Crashing through the underbrush she arrived at the clearing where Gilbert sat with the horses. She stopped running and bent over, her hands on her knees. She stood, putting her hands on her hips and began to walk slowly around the clearing, waiting for her breathing to return to normal.

"Fliss is cute," she said as she bent forward, placing her palms on the ground.

"She is attractive. Her sister Constance, though, appears to be more…accommodating."

"You better be careful, Grunt. We are in a foreign land,

guests of a powerful man. I would hate to see you leave these lands as a eunuch."

"Ouch, don't even say that." He put his hands over his crotch and looked at her with horror.

Tig laughed. "I don't want you to get in any trouble, that's all."

She finished her stretches and went to Juno, pulling her sword free of the saddle. She walked up to Gilbert, and poked him with her sword. "Come on, spar with me."

Gilbert, sprang to his feet, pulled his sword, and, without hesitation, attacked her, hoping to catch her off guard and perhaps gain an advantage that would see him win this fight.

Tig was ready. She met his every parry and thrust. They moved around the clearing, Gilbert advancing on Tig and then Tig pressing him and pushing him back. Gilbert thrust his sword toward her, she met his blade with hers. Steel slid on steel. They stood face to face, their crossed swords between them.

"Let's call it a stalemate, shall we?" Gilbert asked.

Tig quickly stepped back, bringing her sword down. "Agreed." She walked toward Juno and sheathed her sword. "We should get back," she said.

They mounted and turned their horses back toward the estate.

Gilbert was in the salon flirting with the Earl's daughter, Constance, when Simon and the Earl returned from their fishing expedition. Gilbert was sitting beside her, a little too close, and she was laughing at his story. Constance saw Simon as he entered the salon. She stopped laughing, stood and curtsied. Gilbert threw him a look of annoyance.

Simon raised his eyebrow in response. "Where is she?" he asked.

"She is about, Sire. Our ride this morning was a pleasant diversion."

Simon nodded his head, turned on his heel and continued to his room.

"What was that about?" Constance asked.

Gilbert took her hand in his and raised it to his lips. "You smell heavenly, Constance. I wonder, though, do you taste as good as you smell?" He leaned toward her with the intention of stealing a kiss.

"You rogue," she exclaimed as she pushed him away. "You will have to try harder than that to win a kiss from me."

"Let us hope that is the only prize he is after," Mary said as she entered the salon.

Constance and Gilbert turned in surprise at her appearance.

"Mistress, how pleasant that you have joined us," Gilbert said as he bowed to her.

"No, it is not, sir, but I am here nonetheless," Mary responded. She sat in a chair by the window, picking up a frame and began to work on the needlepoint stretched across its bars.

Gilbert and Constance took seats across from each other at a table and began to play cards.

• • •

Tig was bored. Her days at Moregane were filled with training men and her fitness routine. Her days at the Inn were filled with serving customers and cleaning. Her options here were very limited. She had never been interested in fashion and she was not a party girl. Nor was she consumed with making a good match and marrying.

She spent time with Juno, she played with Griffin, she toured the grounds, and she explored the library. She found an atlas on the shelves in the library and lost herself in examining its pages. She found Moregane and was surprised to see just how large it was. She searched for and found Skree, Freecourt, Sandria, and Barring.

She was pulled away from her examination by the chiming of a clock. She had not realized how late it was. She closed the atlas and went to her room. She opened the door to find Simon sitting in a chair in front of the hearth with a glass of whiskey in his hand. She went to him and took the glass, taking a swallow. He took her hand and pulled her onto his lap. She leaned against him.

"How was your fishing expedition?" she asked.

"You will be eating the fruits of our labor this evening."

"What do you think of the Earl?"

"He seems to be an honorable man. He is an interesting companion, as well, good company. How was your day?"

"It was wonderful to go for a run! I sparred with Gilbert as well. I decided to let him win and not run him through."

"I am grateful for that, Tig." He chuckled. "I rely on him quite a bit."

"As do I, Simon. He is a good friend to me."

She took his hand in hers and together they sat in silence, sharing the last of the whiskey in the glass.

Supper was delicious, the conversation light and entertaining. Fliss stole glances at Gilbert throughout the meal while he flirted shamelessly with Constance. After the meal the men retired to the study to share cigars and liquor. Again, the ladies sat in the salon. Constance and Mary gossiped about the people they knew. Fliss had her nose stuck in a book.

Tig stayed with them for a short time and then excused herself. She walked through the garden with Griffin before returning to her room. She washed up and climbed into bed with every intention of waiting for Simon. Instead, she fell asleep and did not stir when he climbed into bed and pulled her to his side.

CHAPTER 24

She woke the next morning to find Simon dressed, sitting on a chair and pulling on his boots.

"Where are you going?" she asked groggily.

"The Earl and I will be hunting today. There will be fresh game for supper tonight," he said as he walked to the bed, leaned over, and kissed her. "Behave yourself today, Lady Tig."

"As you command, Sire." She smiled at him.

"I cherish your obedience, madam," he said as he picked up his jacket and left the room.

Tig lay in bed trying to formulate a plan for her day. Several options came to mind, breakfast being the first of them.

Fliss greeted Tig when she entered the dining room. While Tig placed her breakfast order, Fliss read for a short time and then inserted the ribbon in her book before closing it. As if on cue, Gilbert joined them for breakfast.

"Did you have a pleasant evening?" Fliss asked to no one in particular.

"Indeed I did," Gilbert replied.

Fliss turned a bright shade of red, then turned to Tig.

"As did I, Fliss, thank you," Tig responded. "How is

your book? Is it entertaining? Would you recommend it to me?"

"It is not a work of fiction," she responded, "it is most informative though. I am enjoying it, but I don't know if it is the type of book you would read."

"Tell us then," Gilbert said. "What is it about?"

"It is an account of General Dunsmuir's siege of Furlington."

Of all the topics they might have guessed, this was the furthest from their minds. Tig exchanged a look of surprise with Gilbert, who turned to Fliss with interest. Fliss however was looking down at her hands, her cheeks still red.

"The General's account?" Gilbert asked.

"Yes, he speaks in the first person," Fliss responded.

"Then I imagine you can discount a great deal of what is written there. The General thinks quite highly of himself."

"You know the General?" There was excitement in Fliss' voice.

"I have met him several times."

"Is he brilliant? He is a magnificent strategist from what I can tell."

"As I said, he thinks quite highly of himself. He is surrounded by a very capable staff. I would suggest that perhaps they are owed a large share of credit for his success."

"Perhaps you underestimate him," Fliss suggested.

"I think not, Lady Fliss. I must say that he does cut a fine figure in his uniform and that is what really matters to most ladies, is it not?"

Tig kicked him under the table.

Fliss' mouth dropped open. She stood abruptly, picking up the book and held it to her chest. "I believe, sir, that you are given to exaggeration. I will tell you this however, that you have greatly underestimated me. You cut a fine figure in your attire and you matter not at all to me." She turned and marched out of the room.

"That could have gone better, Grunt," Tig said.

"Dunsmuir is an absolute ass," he responded. "I don't believe a single word of that book is true. If she ever did meet the man she would be greatly disappointed."

"What are the chances that she will meet him?"

"I'd say very slim in this backwater."

"Exactly. And now you are making her question her opinion of a man that she admires."

"I should apologize, I suppose."

"You suppose correctly, Grunt."

Their breakfasts arrived and talk turned to plans for the day.

After breakfast Tig saddled Juno and rode out. Her plans were to return to the clearing she and Gilbert had found the day before. She had her sais and stars with her and would be practicing with those.

Back at the estate, Gilbert found Fliss in the library. She looked up when he entered and then quickly returned to her book.

"I come in peace, Lady Fliss," he said.

She placed the ribbon in her book and closed it.

Gilbert stood in front of her. He held out a book to her.

"This is mine. It is an account of Admiral Perlov's years of fighting pirates on the high seas. I have read it several times and find it both informative and enjoyable."

"Have you met the Admiral?"

"I have. Look here," he opened the cover of the book, "he has inscribed it for me."

Gingerly she took the book from his hands and read the inscription. "Thank you," she said. "I am sure that I will enjoy it. I shall start reading it right away. I will have it back to you before you leave."

"Do not worry, it is yours if you do not finish it."

"That is most generous, sir."

"You may call me Gilbert."

Her eyes sparkled as she looked at him, a blush rising on her cheeks. Gilbert was experienced enough to know that she was attracted to him, but she was such an innocent. Her sister Constance, however, there was fun that could be had there.

Again, Simon and the Earl did not return to the estate until late in the day. Boar would be served tonight.

Tig was in the library again, having found a book of bawdy short stories. The stories were suggestive and her body reacted to the words that she read. She was looking forward to being alone with Simon and working off the tension that was building in her. She had just finished an especially steamy story when she slammed the book shut and went to their room.

She opened the door and found Simon sitting on the

bed having just removed his boots. He looked up as she entered, meeting her eyes. He knew immediately what she wanted. He smiled and sadly shook his head.

"I have had a long day, Tig, and it is not even close to being over."

She stopped and looked at him, disappointment on her face. "You are not serious, are you, Simon?"

"I am," he responded simply.

She smiled slyly, approaching him. She took his hand, lifted her skirt and placed it between her legs. "I am ready," she groaned as she rubbed herself on him. "It won't be much work for you."

"Tig, please," he said as he pulled his hand away. "Not now, not tonight."

"For fuck's sake," she blurted as she turned her back on him.

"I am more than just a cock for you to play with whenever you want."

"Unfortunately for me," she snapped.

"Come on, Tig, how often have I denied you." He was annoyed at her attitude.

"I don't care. I want you now," she argued.

"Your attitude is not advancing your case."

She turned to him, "I knew I should have stayed at the Inn. Mathan was more than willing to let me use his cock." She knew it was a mistake to have said that the minute the words left her mouth.

Simon looked at her, his eyes narrowed, his lips drawn in a tight line. "Is that so?"

"Yes." She knew she should stop but she couldn't. "Morning, noon and night."

He pushed his boots on, stood and grabbed his jacket. "Perhaps I was the one who made the mistake in bringing you with me." He left the room. He didn't even want to look at her right now, much less fuck her.

Dinner that night was unbearable for Tig. Simon totally ignored her. Instead, he flirted with Mary, laughing at her quips, seeming to be intensely interested in everything she said. Gilbert was still wooing Constance, who seemed to be softening toward his advances.

The Earl sat at the head of his table with the look of a cat having swallowed a canary. His eldest daughter seemed to have caught the attention of the king, at last. His middle daughter was captivating the king's emissary. Could this be two advantageous matches? He certainly hoped so.

She was not alone in her misery, however. Fliss was too timid to try to divert Gilbert's attention to her. Tig commiserated with her but was too wrapped up in her own misery to offer her any entertainment.

Simon did not share her bed that night, which made their argument even worse. Where was he? Who was he with? What were they doing? Those questions and the possible answers to them ran through her mind all night long, denying her a restful sleep.

She woke the next morning feeling tired. She lay in bed, those same questions and answers nagging her. She closed her eyes again and fell asleep.

When she woke several hours later Simon was there, watching her, waiting for her to wake up.

He sat with his elbows resting on his knees, his hands clasped together. "What was it about that man, Tig, beside his cock, of course, that made you pick him?"

Tig slid up against the headboard, pulling the blanket up to cover her nakedness. "He was kind and gentle. He had a huge heart."

"Well, you certainly didn't waste any time, did you? We were apart for what, three, four months."

"Meaning what? As far as I knew, you were married. Married and fucking Sophie. What did I have to wait for? My life didn't end because you decided to marry her."

"I had hoped that you would not have found it so easy to replace me."

"He wanted to marry me."

"Gods! We have been separated twice Tig and each time you have found someone to marry you. Is there any man that doesn't want to marry you?"

"Yes, several men, as a matter of fact."

"Really? Who? Who is this paragon of strength? Who is the man with a heart of stone who does not want to marry you?"

"You. You don't want to marry me. Also Gilbert. He has not proposed yet."

Simon jerked at her response. Why had he not proposed to her? Why had he not made her his queen? It would have solved a lot of problems if she had been bound to him.

"Does that bother you, Tig, that I have not proposed to you?" he asked softly.

"Only when you decide to marry other women," she snapped.

"I'm glad you turned him down," he said in a conciliatory tone.

"He didn't want his children to be born bastards," she said.

Simon stood abruptly and stormed toward the bed. "Are you carrying his child?" It had never occurred to him that that had been a possibility.

"No. I don't want children. Not right now, anyway. But once I turned him down, he cut off all access to his cock."

Relief washed over him that she was not pregnant. That last statement, though, a final twist to his guts with her knife. He would make her pay for that.

He sat beside her on the bed and took her hand in his. He lifted it to his lips and kissed it. He turned her hand over and kissed her palm, then her wrist, her elbow, her shoulder. He nuzzled her neck and then claimed her lips. He pulled the blanket away from her, nuzzling her neck again and then kissing her collarbone, in between her breasts. He sucked one nipple into his mouth, swirling his tongue around it, then the other nipple.

Tig was melting. Her want was building with his every kiss. She rose to her knees and straddled him. Simon slid his hands down her back and cupped her ass, pulling her against him. He returned to her lips, increasing his pressure. He pushed her down, spreading her legs and laying on top of her. He slid down her body, licking and kissing her stomach, then her navel. He opened her legs and licked her wetness, circling her clit.

Tig lifted her hips, burying his face in her softness. She was moaning. He began his slow trail up her body, nipping her nipples and claiming her lips once again. He propped himself up on his elbows looking down at her half-closed eyes, listening to her panting. She wriggled against him, asking him to take her.

He stood, looking down at her. She put her hand out to him, to pull him back. He stepped back from her. "Supper will be ready by now. I'm hungry." He turned toward the door.

Realization that he was going to leave her in this state on purpose hit her like a blast of cold air. She sat up, grabbed a vase, and hurled it at him. The door closed on her scream of rage.

CHAPTER 25

It had been two days since Simon had left her wanting. Tig had stayed in their room the whole time. Simon had found a bed elsewhere.

He had felt pretty satisfied with himself as he walked away from her and went to dinner. By the time dinner was done, he felt like a fool. He had been interested in her relationship with Mathan, about what she had seen in him and why she had been with him. He wanted to know, but, then again, he didn't. She was his and he didn't like sharing.

She had been frustrated and had baited him with talk of Mathan's cock. When she had brought up the possibility of children, it had hit him that she had *really* been sharing herself with Mathan and images of her being plowed by this other man angered him. He knew what they shared was special. He doubted that Mathan had been able to satisfy her as he could. But, he was human. He should have chided her, made a joke. Instead, he had punished her. This was just one more mark against him.

She was volatile and he loved her for it. She kept him on his toes. And when she forgave him, when she surrendered to him, it was pure heaven. She was a drug and he was addicted. He was hers, body and soul. They were leaving tomorrow morning. He would have to face her tonight. He anticipated it and dreaded it at the same time.

• • •

Tig was feeling much the same. Simon had denied her and rightly so if he was tired. He was much more than a cock. She wanted to hurt him for denying her and leaving her wanting. She knew it was wrong for her to speak about Mathan's cock and almost as soon as the words were out of her mouth she wanted to take them back, but she didn't, and then she had continued. She should have expected Simon to react the way that he had but she hadn't. She was not surprised that he had avoided her for the past two days. She would have to speak to him today. She would have to ask for his forgiveness.

Across the hall, Gilbert was gathering his things and packing. He was happy. He had finally broken down Constance's resistance. After supper he had convinced her to stroll through the garden with him. He had pulled her behind a hedge and stolen the kiss he had wanted from first meeting her. She had allowed him to kiss her and she had returned his kiss with passion.

He had pushed her breast over the low neckline of her dress and claimed a nipple. He had licked it and sucked it until she begged him for more. He pushed her other breast up and teased her other nipple. She had arched her back, shoving her breasts into his face. He kissed her again before returning to her nipples. He slid his hand under her dress, up her thigh and in between her legs. She moaned as he teased her. He was about to lay her down on the grass when Mary had called her name.

They both froze.

"Oh, no," she gasped as she pushed Gilbert away from her.

"Constance, where are you?" Mary called again. She was coming nearer.

Constance tugged on the neckline of her dress, leaning forward and shoving her breasts back into place. Gilbert smoothed down her skirt. She put her hand up to her hair.

Gilbert was straightening his jacket as Mary turned the corner.

She studied them. "Looks like I arrived just in time," she said dryly.

"Whatever are you talking about, Mary?" Constance chided. "We were just admiring the garden before returning to the house, weren't we, Gilbert?"

"Yes, we were," he responded.

Mary rolled her eyes. "You overstep yourself, Sir," she said to Gilbert before turning back toward the house. "Come along, Constance. You can thank me later for my timely arrival."

Gilbert would think about Constance for some time, the one that got away. If he had another three days.... There was a knock on his door. He opened it to find Fliss standing in the hallway.

"I've finished your book, Gilbert," she said as she held out her hand, offering him the book.

"Did you enjoy it, Fliss?"

"I did. It was like an adventure novel. I find it hard to believe that it is true."

He took the book from her. "That is because you are so innocent, Fliss." He smiled at her.

"Not so innocent as you think, Gilbert," she said as she stepped forward and kissed him on the lips.

Gilbert was taken by surprise. He pulled away from her, looking down at her. She returned his gaze. She looked down and then back up into his eyes. She licked her lips.

Gilbert didn't think twice, he dropped the book on the floor, took her in his arms and kissed her passionately. Fliss wrapped her arms around his neck, pressing herself against him as she returned his kiss.

As he kissed her, Gilbert had several thoughts run through his mind at the same time: she is a child, he should have spent more time with her, she had an amazing effect on his body and his mind. That first thought popped back into his mind, she is a child. He put his hands on her shoulders and gently pushed her away from him.

"Don't say anything, please," Fliss said. "I know you prefer Constance. I know you are leaving tomorrow and I will never see you again." She looked away and then back at him again, tears were shining in her eyes. "Don't forget me." She turned and ran away from him.

Simon entered their room. It was late and he was hoping that Tig was asleep. She wasn't. She was waiting for him. She sat in front of the fire, her head resting on the back of the chair. He came and stood in front of her.

"I have been such a fool, Simon. Forgive me," she whispered.

"Always," he said softly as he reached out and placed his hand on her cheek. He bent down and kissed her. "How can I not?"

Tig stood and walked into his arms. He held her tightly, his chin resting on the top of her head, all tension leaving his body.

CHAPTER 26

Three months later they were back in Moregane. The remainder of their trip, although a long journey, had been pleasant and relaxed, but they were all glad to have finally arrived home. Within days they were back into their normal routines.

Tig had just finished her run and her stretches. She instructed the men on the exercises they were to do, when a page ran into the arena to Tig.

"Lady Tig," he said breathlessly, "the king has requested you meet him in his chamber."

Tig was instantly concerned. He had never interrupted her training before. "Is he all right?" she asked.

"I do not know. I have just been sent to fetch you," he said.

Tig immediately left the arena and went to their room. She opened the door and saw Simon sitting in a chair, his back to the door. She closed the door and turned toward him, "Simon, what is wrong?" she asked as she walked toward him.

"Lady Tig," he said.

She passed the chair and looked at him. He was naked, his erection jutting forward.

"Service your king and you shall receive a great reward," he said with a smile.

Tig laughed. "A great reward? What reward is being offered?" She knelt before him, and kissed the tip of his cock. "A bag of gold?"

"No," Simon placed his hand on her head, "even better."

She licked her lips, took the head of his cock in her mouth and slid it out. "A stable of fine horses?"

"No, even better," he exhaled.

"A castle with a full staff?"

He closed his eyes. "Even better, my lady."

"What could be better than those?" She slid him all the way into her mouth and withdrew him slowly, gently sucking. "What reward would be sufficient for my services?"

"You will be rewarded…" he gasped as she gripped the base of his cock and squeezed, "with unlimited access to the royal cock."

She slid him halfway into her mouth, sucking harder, then stopped. She opened her mouth and raised her head, looking at him. "Unlimited access," she asked as she smoothly stroked his cock.

"Yes," he said. He gripped the arms of the chair.

"No reservations?" she asked as she roughly moved her hand up and down his shaft.

"None."

"I will need time to consider your offer, Sire." She bent forward again, swirling her tongue around the hole of his cock while roughly stroking him.

"I demand your immediate answer, madam," he ground out.

"I accept your terms, Sire," she said before taking him into her mouth again.

Simon watched as she sucked him, watched his cock slide in and out of her mouth, but there was a problem. Tig was still clothed.

He reached out and stopped her. He stood and pulled her to her feet. His hands, steady and strong, ripped the clothes from her body. He turned her and steered her backward toward the bed. Her thighs hit the edge of the mattress. He threw her down, grabbed her legs, spreading them apart and thrust into her. Tig screamed with pleasure, reaching up and burying her hands in his hair. He took her wrists in his hands and held them over her head on the bed.

He grunted as he thrust into her again and again. Tig took each thrust, pushing her pelvis upward, meeting him. She spread her legs wider apart, allowing him to delve deeper within her. He thrust forward and upward, rubbing her clit with each stroke.

Her body tensed, her legs wrapped around his waist, restricting his movement. He pulled her legs apart continuing his assault, plunging into her, rubbing her clit.

Tig thought she was going to lose her mind. Her nipples were erect and tingling, her clit was throbbing, her pussy was wet and dripping. Simon held her legs apart, giving her clit ceaseless stimulation. She came hard, her pussy gripping his cock. He continued to pound into her, continued to rub her clit. Waves of pleasure overtook her. Her back arched, she held her breath. He thrust into her again and again until he finally reached his climax. He grabbed her hips and pulled her tighter onto his cock, the veins in his neck bulged, his face red, his cock shooting his seed into her.

He threw himself down beside her, panting from exertion. Tig lay still gasping as the waves of pleasure subsided.

"Sire," she said.

"Ummmm."

"I just need some clarification."

"What?"

"By the royal cock, do you mean this cock," she asked as she placed her hand on him.

He rolled onto his side, looking into her eyes. He reached up and took her nipple in his fingers, twisting it.

Tig gasped.

He twisted her nipple again. "I do. I assure you, madam, that it is most adequate and up to the task of rewarding you again and again."

She felt him stir back to life under her hand. "I agree with you, Your Highness. Thank you for your clarification."

He took her other nipple in his fingers, squeezing and twisting it. "You are welcome, madam."

Tig began to squirm. The sensation from her nipples sent an electric current directly to her pussy.

Simon released her nipple and slid his hand down her belly and in between her legs. She was wet and slippery. He found her nub and rubbed it slowly. It began to harden. He moved his fingers down, gliding over her. He slid his fingers into her, fucking her slowly.

His erection had returned. He pulled his fingers out of her, sat up and pulled her up onto his lap, his cock easily slid into her. He held her hips against him, her ass pushed into his stomach, as he slowly moved in her. She started to move with him. He brought his hands up to her breasts, squeezing and massaging them before taking her nipples in his fingers, squeezing them and twisting them.

Tig leaned back against him. He nuzzled her neck, relentlessly squeezing and twisting her nipples. He stuck his tongue into her ear. She screamed again, wanting more and began to bounce up and down on his cock. She placed her hands on his. He squeezed her nipples and twisted them harder. She was beyond thought. All she wanted was more. She spread her legs wider, urging Simon to pump faster. She arched her back and lifted her arms, linking her fingers behind his neck.

Simon continued to mercilessly squeeze and twist her nipples. He quickened his pace, thrusting into her while thrusting his tongue in and out of her ear.

Tig came with a scream at the moment that Simon ejaculated into her. He fell back on the bed, taking her with him. She began to hum and continued to writhe, she ran her hands over her body, rubbing her sensitive nipples, down between her legs and back up again, her eyes half closed.

"I want some of that," Simon whispered into her ear.

She quickly lifted herself and fell on top of him. She rubbed her body against his, her nipples gliding across his chest, her pussy grinding into his crotch. He ran his hands up and down her back, enjoying the sensation of her body rubbing and pushing into him while she hummed with pleasure.

Tig stopped writhing. She was warm and tingling. Simon rolled to his side. She slid off of him. She pulled her arms across her breasts and threw her leg over his. He pulled her into him, nestling her head against his chest, his chin resting on top of her head. He slid his hand down her back and up again. They fell asleep wrapped in each other.

They woke in the late afternoon.

"Are you hungry," Simon asked.

Tig smiled. "Depends. What's on the menu?"

He laughed and pointed. She noticed plates of food set out on the table.

"You! You planned this whole thing?"

He kissed her nose. "I did." He ran his fingers across her collarbone. "Are you hungry?"

"Famished."

He got out of bed, leaving her cozy underneath the covers. He picked up a plate, selected some meats, cheese, bread and fruit, and carried it back to her.

She pushed herself up, leaning against the headboard. He picked up a piece of chicken and brought it to her lips. She opened her mouth and he fed it to her. He tore off a small piece of bread and fed that to her as well.

"I do believe this is the best meal I have ever eaten," she said.

"Remember our picnic in the mountains?" he asked.

"I do. It was a warm spring day."

"Yes, the sun was shining and the flowers were beginning to bloom."

He picked up a wedge of cheese and took a bite. He got up and returned to the table, pouring a glass of whiskey which he brought back to bed. He took a sip and passed the glass to Tig. She took a sip and returned the glass to him.

"You told me the story about your first love," she snickered.

"Yes, the lovely Isabel," he grinned. "I was very young." He took a piece of meat and popped it into his mouth. "Who knew that the gift of a lizard was not a token of love?"

"Tell me again about when you gave it to her?" she asked, still smiling.

"It was a beauty, Tig. I had caught it that morning. It was green with huge yellow eyes. I put it in a box and tied it with a ribbon. She would know how much I loved her when she opened it. I was sure. I found her in the woods where we would play and I gave it to her. My heart was thumping. Would she open the box and kiss me?" Simon looked at her with anticipation on his face.

Tig giggled and slid down the headboard. "Did she kiss you?"

"No! She smiled when I gave it to her and she thanked me. I don't know what she was expecting, but she was excited. I could almost taste her lips on mine. I didn't know what would happen after she kissed me but I was looking forward to finding out." He paused, took a sip of whiskey and continued. "She untied the box and opened it. The lizard saw his freedom and jumped out of the box, onto her arm and raced up into her hair. She screamed and began to jump around hitting her head trying to dislodge the poor lizard."

Tig was laughing.

"I was more concerned about the lizard! The poor thing was about to be pounded to death. I knew that if she didn't like the lizard she would be even less pleased with lizard guts in her hair. She was wailing by this time. I managed to grab the lizard out of her hair and held it out to her in my hand to show her that I had it. She screamed again and slapped my hand away from her, sending the lizard flying into the woods." He looked at Tig with confusion on his face, as if, to this day, he could not comprehend the failure of his lizard gift. "She hated me after that and refused to come anywhere near me."

"Poor you," Tig sympathized with him.

"I have learned a lot since then, though, Tig. No more lizard gifts for the ladies." He grinned rakishly.

"Not even for me?"

"No, not even for you. For you, I have a snake." He pointed down to his crotch, his cock was coming to life before her eyes. "A big snake."

Tig howled.

"You laugh at my gift?"

She couldn't speak she was laughing so hard. Her eyes began to water. She slid down from the headboard onto the bed.

Simon smiled down at her. He placed the plate of food on the floor beside the bed, he drained the whiskey and placed the glass down as well. He slid down and lay beside her. He propped himself up on his elbow, watching the laughter leave her face as he ran his fingers lightly around her neck, down between her breasts and back again. They gazed into each other's eyes, love and lust intermingled. "You are my gift," he said as he leaned down and kissed her gently.

Tig placed her hand on his cheek, returning his kiss.

Simon lifted himself off the bed and slid under the covers with her. He pulled her to him again and gave her a long passionate kiss. He rolled her onto her back and entered her slowly. He lay with his cock in her, kissing her again and again. He began to move within her, slowly and gently. "You are my treasure," he whispered.

Tig wrapped her legs around him, taking him in. She was warm and happy. She pushed him up, watching his face and his eyes as he took her. He returned her gaze as he silently thrust into her. The climax built slowly and washed over both of them powerfully, leaving them breathless.

CHAPTER 27

Weeks later, Tig returned to the castle. She and the men had been doing drills on horseback on the plain. It was late in the day. She entered the castle to find Mrs. Abbot waiting for her.

"The King has asked that you go to your tower room. He has a gift for you there. We have a special visitor coming for dinner and he wants you to prepare yourself," she said in a rush.

Tig was immediately on edge. "What visitor? Who is coming?"

"He would not say. I don't know. He just asked that you clean yourself up. There is a bath waiting for you. I will send a girl to do your hair," she responded. She should have stopped at that but could not help herself from adding, "Please don't hurt her."

"I won't hurt her," Tig responded angrily. Mrs. Abbot so annoyed her. "Where is Simon?" The last time this exact situation occurred, the special guest was Sophie. Was he bringing another betrothed to the castle? She would kill him this time if that were so.

"I don't know that either, Lady Tig. You will need time to prepare," she hinted.

Tig glared at her and then stalked toward Simon's

office. The doors were open and she entered to find John alone, transcribing the day's dictation.

"Where is he, John?" Tig asked, unable to keep the edge from her voice.

"I do not know, Lady Tig."

"Who is coming for dinner? Who is the special guest?"

"I do not know that either, Madam. All he said was that there was to be a wedding tonight."

"A wedding," she shrieked.

"Yes."

"Who's wedding?"

"His, I think."

Tig's world stopped. A red haze dropped over her eyes. She was going to kill him. She was going to kill him and she would feel no remorse. She spun on her heel and left his office. How dare he. She began her search for him. She went directly to their chamber. He was not there. She looked for him in every other room in the castle, including the kitchen. Her broken heart was being replaced by stony resolve. She would find him and kill him. She left the castle and went to the stables, then the garden. No amount of his charm would save him from her vengeance this time.

She couldn't find him anywhere. So, he had left a gift for her in her room. What did he possibly think would buy her compliance? She would see. Whatever it was, it wasn't enough.

She entered her room and there, on a dress form, was probably the most beautiful dress she had ever seen. Yards of pale pink silk gathered to form a voluminous skirt below a corset of the same pale pink. There was silver edging emphasizing the seams of the corset with delicate white roses embroidered at the neck. The sleeves were fitted and came to a point that would end in the middle of her hand.

She pulled a knife and strode toward the dress. She was going to shred it. Beautiful as it was, it was not payment enough to buy her compliance. She would shred the dress. Then she would find Simon and kill him. She lifted the knife, ready to bring it down in a ripping strike. And then she stopped.

No. She would do as he asked. She would clean herself up, have her hair done and put on the damned dress. She would sit through his wedding to whatever cunt he had chosen this time and then she would fucking kill him. She smiled then. It was a perfect plan.

She bathed and dried herself. She slid on the white stockings and tied them with the pale pink ribbon that sat beside them. She lifted a sheer silk slip over her head, adjusted it and tied it.

There was a knock at her door. She opened it and allowed a young girl to enter before slamming the door behind her. She glared at the girl. "Let's get on with it, then."

The girl cowered away from her, then straightened. She came toward Tig. With trembling fingers, she undid the tie on Tig's shift, opening the neck and letting it plunge to just above her nipples. "For the dress, Milady," she stuttered. She picked up the embroidered corset from the bed. Tig held it against her as the girl tightened and tied it in the back.

The girl went to the dress. She slid her hands under the skirt and lifted it off the form, sliding her hands under the bodice to the neck. She turned with it and held it out to Tig. Tig bent, pushing her arms through the sleeves and her head through neckline. She stood. The girl walked around her, adjusting the dress on her shoulders and her waist, smoothing the skirt down. She tightened the laces and stood back, eyeing Tig, checking the fit, and made minor adjustments.

She motioned Tig toward a stool. Before she sat, the girl lifted her skirt so she would not sit on the dress. Tig endured the next hour, her blood boiling, going over her plan to kill Simon, revising it, refining it. Her hair was done in long blond curls and then arranged on her head with jeweled pins. Perfume was dabbed behind her ears, in the hollow of her neck and at her wrists. Her eyes were lined and brushed with a light pink pigment. Her cheeks as well. Her lips highlighted with pink.

At last the girl stood back and looked at Tig. She nodded her head, went to the door and opened it. A valet entered, carrying a large royal blue case. The girl opened it and lifted out a diamond collar. She put it on Tig's neck and fastened it. She returned to the case and pulled out a necklace, heavy with more diamonds. That was fastened to Tig's neck as well. Next were two diamond drop earrings and a bracelet.

That valet left and a second valet entered carrying another royal blue case. The girl opened it and lifted up a diamond tiara. She arranged it in the curls piled on Tig's head. The valet left the room. The girl picked up a pair of pale pink slippers and slid them onto Tig's feet. She held out her hand to Tig. Tig took her hand and stood. Once again, she circled Tig, adjusting, smoothing, pulling. At last, she stood back to admire her work. She gasped. "You are beautiful Milady. You will leave the king breathless when he sees you," she gasped.

"I will leave him breathless all right," she snapped. The fact that she had been draped in diamonds escaped her notice. When the girl spoke and she looked at herself in a mirror she was pleased with the results. At least she will die dressed in finery. Oh yes, she fully expected that she would not live long after she plunged her knife into Simon's heart.

The girl opened the door to the tower and stood back. Tig left the room and descended the stairs. Waiting for her at the bottom of the stairs was Gilbert. He was dressed in velvet pants and jacket, a gold brocade vest and a blinding white silk shirt. He gaped at the sight of her and then bowed with a flourish. "Lady Tig, you are magnificent," he said.

Of course, Simon would send Gilbert for her. He knew that she would never harm him. He no doubt had orders to try to appease her and control her as she sat through this farce of a ceremony.

Gilbert stood and offered his arm to her. She grabbed it, more forcefully than she intended.

"Relax. This is a happy day," he said as he placed his hand on hers.

The girl who had dressed her came running down the stairs, past them, and around the corner to the common room. Tig noticed that there were no other people in the halls. Of course, they were all in the common room waiting for the wedding to begin!

Gilbert led her down the hall, chatting about gods knew what. Tig was focused on her plan, still refining the minor details. They neared the common room. She could hear the muted buzz of conversation and string instruments being played.

They turned the corner and Gilbert lead her to the middle of the entranceway. Suddenly the music stopped and all conversation ceased. Tig looked up. The people stood and turned to her. She was at the head of an aisle. The common room was decorated with huge vases of pink and red roses, the tables laden with food. The people, not all of whom she recognized, were dressed in their finest. She looked down the length of the aisle.

At the end stood Simon. He was dressed in royal blue velvet, a sash of red crossed his body, an ornamental sword and sheath hung from his belt. He was looking at her, wearing a broad smile.

It hit her then, the dress, the jewels—this was her wedding! Simon was going to marry her. She laughed. She would kill him...but later. Much, much later. She was positive more than one incident would arise in their lives together that he would be lucky to live through.

Gilbert took a step forward, pulling her with him and refocusing her thoughts to the present. Music began to play as he led her down the aisle to Simon. He took her hand from his arm, placed it in Simon's hand and stepped back to stand beside Simon.

Simon took her other hand in his and gazed into her eyes. "Will you marry me, Tig?" he whispered as the minister began to speak.

"If you insist," she whispered.

"Your king commands it." He smiled gently at her.

"Who am I to disobey an order from my king?" she replied with a smirk.

They were focused on each other, the ceremony seeming to be held in some other place. It felt like mere moments before Simon was leaning forward to brush his lips against hers. Then he dropped her hands and pulled her into a fierce embrace, bending her slightly backward and kissing her passionately. Applause broke out.

The meal was sumptuous, the music happy and lively. Tig and Simon mingled with the guests and danced. Simon was speaking to someone when Gilbert appeared before her. He bowed to her. "Your Highness, may I have this dance?" he asked.

"Please, Grunt, call me Tig."

"No, I will not. You are my queen now," he stopped and smiled at her, "but you will always be my dear friend."

She smiled and kissed him on the cheek.

"Lips off Gilbert, Madam," Simon said behind her. "Those are for the king's enjoyment alone."

They all laughed. A waiter appeared with a tray of drinks. They all took a glass of whiskey, held them up, clinked the glasses and drank. Simon put his arm around Tig's waist, pulling her closer to him. Tig turned into his arms and hugged him. He looked down and kissed her on the forehead. "I have promised Grunt a dance," she said.

"Be off with you then," he said.

Simon and Tig danced and talked and laughed until dawn. At last Simon took her hand and led her out of the common room, down the hall to their chamber. He opened the door, allowing her to enter first. Their room was decorated with flowers, plates of food arranged on the table. The bed had been turned down; a single red rose placed on the sheets.

"This will be a first for me, Tig," Simon said.

"Being married?"

"Yes, that, but also," he whispered into her ear, "fucking a queen!"

She laughed. Simon leaned down and kissed her, demanding a response and Tig answered.

Tig was naked, laying in Simon's arms, fully sated. She was warm and cozy, tired but tingling. "Tell me a story, Simon," she said on a yawn.

He kissed the top of her head. "I will tell you about the time I found the love of my life." He felt her body tense. He would have to measure his words carefully. He smiled.

"I met her at a party in Barring," he began. "It was late summer, going into fall. I happened to look up from a conversation with friends and there she was. My breath caught in my throat at the sight of her. My heart almost stopped. I vowed I would find out who she was by the end of the night."

Simon pulled Tig tighter toward him. She had put some distance between them.

"Tell me another story. I don't want to hear the rest of this one."

"Why not? Don't you want to know everything about me?" he teased as he looked down and kissed the tip of her nose. "Besides, I'm getting to the good part."

"Do you honestly think I want to listen to this?" Tig pushed against him. She was getting annoyed.

Simon held her tightly. "Every time I looked up, I found her watching me. She would tip her glass of wine toward me and smile. There was a promise in those smiles and I could hardly wait to take her up on that promise."

"Okay, I get it, you met her, you fucked her, blah blah blah." Tig had had enough of this story.

"If only it had been that simple Tig. I did meet her, she pulled me into the garden but to be honest I would have followed her anywhere."

"Hey. This is starting to sound familiar."

"It should. I was about to claim her lips in another kiss when some men popped out of the bushes and she took me prisoner. She knocked me out, tied me up, and put me on a horse to bring me back to Moregane for execution."

"Really! And you fell in love with her?"

"How could I not? She is beautiful, courageous, loving, gentle. She is everything."

"Everything you want in a woman?"

"No, you are simply everything to me. Every breath I take, every beat of my heart. There is no me without you, Tig."

About Geneva Gordon

Geneva Gordon enjoys all types of fiction. This is her first book which incorporates many genres to create a story that excites her and has combined the elements she has longed to find in one book.

Books by Geneva Gordon
One Task: The Warrior and the King
The Demon You Love (One Task #2)
The King's Treasure (One Task #3)
You Can't Delete You
Say Yes, Baby

Also from Deep Desires Press!

The Frozen Prince
Minna Louche

Genevieve is a mere servant girl for the royal family, who's best friend happens to be the princess, Malaya. When a powerful and dangerous man attacks the castle in an effort to steal the princess, Genevieve acts quickly to save Malaya—by offering herself instead.

The thwarted abductor, however, is no ordinary man. He is the Frozen Prince—a supposed urban legend cursed with an ice-filled heart and dark magic. When Genevieve is swept away to his isolated castle in the Northern Mountain, however, she discovers that there is far more to the legend than has been told. Like the unimaginable depths his ethereal white eyes hold...and the hold they have on her.

Genevieve is trapped between something sinister hiding on the mountain and a cursed prince whose carnal cravings gnaw at his heart. Emblazoned in the icy clutches of desire, if they can't solve the mystery behind the Frozen Prince, neither will survive.

Available in ebook and paperback!

Also from Deep Desires Press

Silk & Swords
Christopher Stires

An alluring young woman damned with a curse challenges the heartless assassin commanded to kill her.

A bereft widow discovers the delights of the marriage bed with a ferocious knight-soldier.

A sensuous female barbarian and her ardent diplomat husband investigate the mysterious murder of a masked prisoner.

Three entwined tales of love and eroticism...tales woven together for the titillation of a powerful, meddling, yet well-meaning queen by a wise, unsettling, sooth-saying oracle.

Plunge into a world where desire and lust rule peasants and royalty alike. Enter the passionate world of Thuria.

Available in ebook and paperback!

Also from Deep Desires Press

Misled by a Monster
Marco May

Mitch has never quite fit in. He's always felt... different somehow, though he could never put his finger on it. When he meets Stan, a strange and mysterious man, he feels an instant attraction and like someone finally truly understands him.

The allure of Stan is so powerful and all-consuming that Mitch soon packs up and leaves everyone behind to move in with Mitch in his rural community. But once ensconced there and separated from everything he used to know, Stan changes. And Mitch is trapped. And there are strange things going on around him...otherworldly things.

Stan's twin brother Wes seems to be Mitch's only hope of escape—and of love. For where Stan is evil, Wes is good. Will Mitch be stuck in misery with Stan? Or is there hope for him and happiness with Wes?

The secrets soon spill and the truth comes out. And the most shocking revelation of all for Mitch? He might not be quite human himself.

Available now in ebook and paperback!